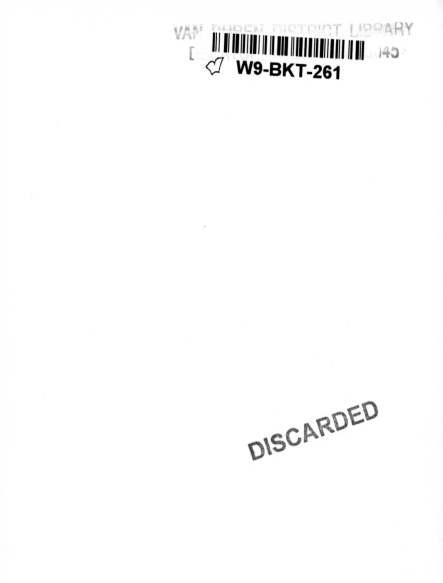

RING AROUND
HIS HEART

Other books by CJ Love:

For the Love of Murphy
A Horse Called Hustle

RING AROUND
HIS HEART

•

CJ Love

AVALON BOOKS
NEW YORK

Lov

Published by Avalon Books,
an imprint of Thomas Bouregy & Co., Inc.
160 Madison Avenue, New York, NY 10016

Library of Congress Cataloging-in-Publication Data

Love, CJ
    Ring around his heart / CJ Love.
        p. cm.
    ISBN 978-0-8034-7794-0 (acid-free paper)   1. Heiresses—
Fiction.   2. Ranchers—Fiction.   3. Marriage—Fiction.
4. Paparazzi—Fiction.   5. Florida—Fiction.   6. Bahamas—
Fiction.   I. Title.
    PS3612.O83385R56 2010
    813'.6—dc22

                                                        2010018319

PRINTED IN THE UNITED STATES OF AMERICA
ON ACID-FREE PAPER
BY HADDON CRAFTSMEN, BLOOMSBURG, PENNSYLVANIA

For my daughter Sarah Cat,
whose hilarity inspires me

Chapter One

Margie pulled her purse off her shoulder and rummaged for her account card. Looking down, she didn't see the man rush through the front entrance of the bank and race toward the stairs. Actually, she never saw him at all, until she bounced off his hard chest.

She sat where she landed on the tile floor. When the man scrambled next to her and began to claw at her bag, Margie squealed, "Get off, *thief!*" while she flailed at him with her open palms.

"Hey, you!" the receptionist shouted. "Stop, you . . . you thug!" Realizing the mugger still clutched her bag, Margie got to her knees to yank at her purse with all her strength.

"You're choking . . . me," he gasped. "You're choking . . ."

The receptionist, who had climbed atop her desk, heaved a candy dish and thumped the man square on the head. Once he lost consciousness, Margie saw that her purse strap was wound tightly around his throat. Gingerly,

1

she lifted the leather and let the man's head fall back against the receptionist's desk. The noise sounded like a hatchet to wood, but Margie didn't have any sympathy for the thief.

"That's what you get for trying to steal my purse."

Five seconds later, Jack came to with his throat aflame. "You lassoed me!"

"What's he mumbling?" a woman's voice asked.

He tried to open his eyes, but the sun streaming through a skylight felt like a knife to his brain. Rolling to his side, Jack growled, "I wasn't trying to steal your purse." His hand found the desk edge and he pulled himself to his feet.

Now he confronted his assailant; he had imagined a pro wrestler had dragged him down, but standing before him was a petite girl, no more than twenty-two or twenty-three years old. She looked slender in her sleeveless blue pantsuit and high-heeled shoes. Golden hair cascaded past her tanned shoulders. Normally, Jack would have found the young woman attractive—beautiful even—but now that she had strangled all fascination for the opposite sex out of him, he saw her for what she really was: a high-fashion boa constrictor.

He watched her green eyes narrow. "You were trying to steal my purse. The strap of it was wrapped around your . . ."

"Neck . . . Yes, it was around my neck."

Her brow wrinkled in confusion.

A familiar voice came from their left. "What's going

on here?" the bank manager demanded. Morris Bonaguide shepherded the girl away from Jack's direct view.
"Are you all right? Has this scoundrel hurt you?"

Jack answered over the blonde's head, "Yes, but I'm
all right now."

"Not you!" Bonaguide bellowed, then bent to see the
girl face to face. "Margie, what happened?"

"She tried to kill me. That's what happened."

The girl twisted around to blink at Jack. She caught
him then, and for a moment he watched her too, completely mesmerized by her emerald eyes. He shook his
head to clear his thoughts. She was a viperess enchanting
her prey! Bonaguide cleared his throat. "Do you have
any idea who you've assaulted? This is Margie . . ."

"Is Brittany still here?" Jack interrupted.

The older man nodded. "That's who you are, you're
with Brittany." He went red about the cheeks. "I'll have
you know she gave no notice."

Jack didn't wait to hear the rest of the man's com-
plaint. He turned toward the stairs and took them by
twos.

Bonaguide's graying hairline raised a fraction and
his dark blue eyes widened. "How rude!"

"Who is he?" Margie asked, still watching the man
climb the stairs. His thick and muscular arms protruded
from the sleeveless plaid shirt he wore over a white
ribbed tee. A gold crucifix swung from his neck and his
longish brown hair flopped as he charged up the steps.

"I don't know his name but I've seen him here before.

He visits one of our accountants." Mr. Bonaguide took Margie's elbow. "One of our *former* accountants. She quit this morning."

"Then he really wasn't trying to steal my purse?"

"Shall I call the police?"

"Oh, no," she insisted. "He said I had lassoed him."

"Lassoed him? Why—?" he started to ask, but then seemed to change his mind. "Do you have business I can help you with today?"

"I only meant to see one of your representatives. You needn't bother."

"I insist," he told her, pointing to a chair in front of his desk. "It's the least I can do after the way you've been treated in our lobby."

Margie looked for her account card again. "I've come for a financial report. I need a list of all my assets and shareholdings."

Bonaguide gave a genuine smile. "Then you and my son have decided to take my advice?" His thin and graying mustache twitched at the corners. "It's quite wise, you know. A prenuptial agreement ensures everyone keeps what he or she started with."

"Yes, Tyler has convinced me to sign."

"You're a smart girl, then. You recognize Tyler has money of his own. Now that he's running for governor he'll need to keep strict accounts." Pulling a keyboard from beneath his desk, Bonaguide typed Margie's account number. Suddenly, he frowned and took a fresh look at her. "I thought you already returned to school."

Margie cleared her throat. "The . . . the dean," she started, trying to make this sound as logical as she could, "thought it would be best if I waited and returned in the fall. That's when the cafeteria will be finished."

"Finished?"

"Being rebuilt."

Bonaguide looked at the ceiling, presumably to consider if he should pursue the subject, and then glanced at Margie again. "What happened to the old cafeteria?"

"It burned down."

"The dean accused you?"

"Well, I . . . I was holding the aerosol can." She might have explained she had only meant to spray Pantene Pro-V flexible hold hair spray into her hair and not in the direction Theresa had lit her cigarette. The hand-held blowtorch had lit the girl's synthetic ponytail on fire. Margie had tried to help but Theresa had raced out of the lavatory leaving mass hysteria in her wake. One of the upper classmen had grabbed the flaming wig and wrapped it in a café curtain, but the draperies had caught fire too. . . .

There it was again, that funny little vein that popped out on Mr. Bonaguide's forehead. "Margie," he began as he laced his fingers on top of his desk. "I hate to bring up an old subject, but as power of attorney over your grandparents' estate, must I consider withholding your inheritance?"

"You're already withholding my inheritance."

"Only until you turn twenty-five, dear." He tried to

smile but didn't quite finish the expression. "Legally, I can hold your funds until you're thirty. It's all written down, you know."

"Unless I marry."

He shut his eyes for a moment. When he opened them again, they were narrow slits of dark blue ice. "If I need to speak to Tyler, I will. I approve of your engagement, of course, but I won't see my son's political career in chaos because you cannot rein in your calamitous nature."

"You would stop the marriage?"

"Delay," he responded in a patient voice. "Delay, Margie. Just like your money, marriage is an enormous responsibility. You must be willing to sacrifice for your husband. Perhaps you're not ready for such commitment."

"Of course I am," she answered, smiling at Uncle Bonny. It was the name she and her sister used to refer to Morris Bonaguide. There was no blood relation whatsoever, but Uncle Bonny was part of the family because he had been so close to Margie's grandparents.

Suddenly, Morris pushed his chair backward and stood. "I guess we'll see, won't we? I'll only be a moment," he told her and walked toward the door.

Margie got to her feet to wait. Crossing her arms, she watched the bank patrons through the glass partition. Her eyes lingered on the stairs and she wondered what happened to the man she had nearly strangled. Perhaps he still searched for his accountant—perhaps he searched for medical attention.

Uncle Bonny emerged from a back room and Margie observed him as he shuffled past the tellers. He was an intense man, always rushing back and forth.

At the same time another man caught her attention. He stood five-deep in the teller line and wore a pin-stripe suit of navy blue. What caught her eye was that he stood in a crooked fashion speaking on a cell phone as he stared straight at Margie. He had tight curly hair and a bushy mustache. He watched her for a moment and then slowly turned around again.

Bonaguide met Margie at the door. "Here you are," he told her, handing her several pages of a report. "I'm sorry we've had to have this little talk today. Will you try to stay out of trouble, dear?"

"Of course."

"Despite what you think, I really have no interest in keeping your money from you. I'm looking out for your best interests."

Margie nodded and smiled at Uncle Bonny. "Yes, I understand."

Margie enjoyed walking in the late morning sunshine. Tall buildings surrounded the landscape and young oak trees emerged in planters all along Eighth Avenue. Red brick inlays dotted the concrete sidewalks. Her cell phone rang and Margie answered it just as she passed a line forming at a street-side egg roll stand.

"I'm at the bakery," her sister, Cat, said on the other end of the line. "What sort of icing do you want on the wedding cake?"

"The sweet kind," Margie told her, stepping around a woman standing in the middle of the sidewalk.

"Buttercream, fondant, or royal icing?"

"Fondant? What's that?"

Cat's voice sounded distant when she held the phone away to ask the clerk the same question. Then she came back with, "He said something about elasticity and smoothness and sugar paste. I don't know though, Margie. I haven't eaten paste since kindergarten."

"Royal icing sounds very stately."

"It has meringue in it. You know I don't like meringue."

Margie grimaced at the crossing signal. "Are you the one getting married?"

"I might as well be. I'm doing all the work."

"Order the buttercream," Margie firmly decided.

"Italian or Swiss?"

"What?"

Just then a man raced past Margie, charged through the red signal of the crosswalk, and then dashed straight into the traffic on Eighth Avenue. A horn blasted as a black Volvo skidded to a stop.

"What's going on?" Cat wanted to know.

"Someone ran headlong into traffic," Margie explained, watching the jaywalker as he slammed his hands on the hood of the car and yelled, "Watch it, pal!"

"You watch it, you lunatic!" the driver hollered right back.

The pedestrian, who was wearing a familiar plaid shirt, didn't stay to argue with the driver and ran toward the opposite sidewalk. A stocky fellow near Margie got in on the exchange. "Where's the fire?" he wanted to know.

"There's a fire?" Cat asked on the other end.

"No, just a jaywalker. Hey, I think it's the guy from the bank."

"Uncle Bonny?"

"No, the good-looking one."

Cat responded, "There is no good-looking one at the bank."

"There was this morning. I lassoed him."

"Should I cancel the wedding cake?"

"Very funny," Margie told her. "Let me think about the icing."

After crossing with the light, Margie found her way to the parking garage. Dimmers lit the first floor. It seemed she was the only person there though she heard the squeal of tires on what had to be the fourth or fifth floor up. Slipping into the black Jaguar XKR coupe, Margie buckled her seat belt and started the engine. With a swift glance in the rearview mirror, she reversed, and plowed backward into a passing Jeep.

Wincing, she carefully opened the door.

"This is great," the other driver burst out. He had jumped from his seat using the roll bar and now stared at the tire and bumper of his vehicle. "This is just great." His long hair fell into his face as he bent to look beneath the tailpipe. When he stood again, he glared at Margie. "You again?"

"Hello," she responded sheepishly.

He ignored her greeting and crouched beside the Jeep.

Margie walked toward him and peered over his shoulder. "It doesn't look too bad," she consoled. "A hammer will bang that dent right out of there."

He jerked around to stare at her. "A hammer? What are you talking about?"

Margie straightened and used her hands to explain. "You know, a piece of wood with an anvil on one end to pound nails."

"I know what a hammer is, but I'm certainly not going to use one on the Jeep."

"Well, it's not like anyone will notice," she pointed out, eyeing his transport. The Jeep had no doors and the metal looked corroded around the gun rack. There was no top to it, just a roll bar, and it had to be the biggest rust bucket Margie had ever seen.

The man placed his hands on his hips, apparently offended by her blatant disdain for his . . . vehicle. "Excuse me?"

"Oh," she answered, trying to cover and playing the moment. She offered her hand in distraction. "Margie."

"The Tampa Strangler, I remember." He regarded her hand without taking it. "Well, Margie, let me thank you for *ruining my life.*"

"It's a dent."

He took a deep breath. "You have no idea what you've done. Pull your car forward so I can find out if the Jeep will run."

"The proper thing to do is notify the authorities." Margie paused then. She sounded just like Uncle Bonny!

The man squinted. With a low voice, he suggested, "The proper thing to do is pull your car forward." He was big and brawny and she was slender and puny, so Margie pulled her car forward.

Out of the vehicle again, she heard him complaining, "I can't drive this. The axle is bent." He eyed Margie. "Hop into the Jeep and steer while I push it out of the way."

Not that he would listen, but Margie objected. "I think we should leave it where it sits. How will the police know who's to blame for the accident?"

"*You're* to blame."

Margie knew he had been speeding and actually took a breath to say so, but he wore such an impatient look that she changed her mind and climbed into the Jeep.

"Take your foot off the brake!" he hollered from behind the Jeep. It seemed to Margie that he hollered a lot.

"My foot is not on the brake," she informed him and then glanced at her foot.

"Anymore."

After a good bit of heaving, the man stopped and then stood beside Margie, right at the doorless front seat, and he reached one muscular arm past her lap to yank the emergency brake. She waited for him to move away, but he didn't. He simply stood there watching her with those very dark brown eyes. In the low light of the garage his angular jaw appeared shadowed and humorless. A tiny scar creased his top lip. Under different circumstances she would have found him rather spectacular. He leaned toward her. "I need you to drive me to the Port of Tampa."

Margie wrinkled her brow. "What?"

"You owe me."

"No, I don't."

"You do." Narrowing his eyes, he took hold of her elbow. "You've destroyed my transportation."

"This battered thing? You weren't going to get far in it anyway. . . ." His eyes grew wide with the effrontery and Margie squeaked her last bit, "I'll call the police."

His expression softened then. "Margie. It is Margie, isn't it?" His dark eyes scanned her features. "Listen, I have to stop Brittany before she boards a ship. It is the most important thing I'll ever do in my life."

Now Margie understood. He was pursuing his love. How romantic. "I can't," she told him. As intriguing as it all sounded, Margie could only see Uncle Bonny's face and his index finger wagging disapprovingly at her.

The man still had her by the arm and now propelled her toward her car. "Drive me," he insisted, "or I'll drive myself." He gazed through the car window. "Ah, the keys are in the ignition."

Margie stepped in front of the door. "You cannot steal my car."

He smiled then, as though he enjoyed the challenge. "Oh, yes I can." He moved right, did a quick step when Margie blocked, and then grabbed the door handle on her left.

"No," she protested, pushing at his bare arm. "I'll drive!" Frustrated, she elbowed past him.

He took a step backward and beamed triumphantly. "You're very generous."

Margie tried to hit him with the car door when she yanked it open but he easily sidestepped and moved around the car to open the passenger door before she could lock it. Blast it all.

"Where do you want to go again?"

He glanced at Margie while buckling his seat belt. "The Port of Tampa. I'll show you the way." Keeping his hands on his faded blue jeans, he tapped his fingers impatiently.

The Jaguar had little damage and started easily. Margie backed out of the parking space and then drove into the bright sunshine.

Neither of them saw the dark blue sedan pull out of the garage behind them.

"Go south on Twenty-First and then make a right on Adamo." Her hijacker stayed silent thereafter except to tell her to change lanes to pass a slow-moving van. Margie glanced at him now and then. His long dark hair tossed in the breeze from the opened window. Thin sideburns grew the length of his ears.

She would feel better about all this if she knew something about him, so she asked, "What's your name?"

"Ivan," he told her without looking at her.

"Ivan? As in Ivan the Terrible? Ivanhoe?"

"As in Jack Ivan. Take a left at Channelside. We should start to see signs . . . there."

Parking in a space overlooking Tampa Bay, Margie unbuckled her seat belt and followed him. A dark blue sedan pulled in and parked next to the Jaguar. Margie didn't see the man with a very large mustache step onto the pavement and flip open his cell phone.

The *Dolphin* cruise ship hoisted anchor and started to slip away from the landing pier. In the brilliant sunlight well-wishers waved good-bye from shore. Twinkling sapphires reflected in the water. Margie squinted to see the travelers gathered on the deck of the ship.

Jack cupped his mouth and shouted, "Brittany!"

Margie shielded her eyes from the sun's glare. "What does she look like?"

"Dark-haired, tall, very pretty . . . Brittany!" He motioned to someone on deck.

Margie looked where he looked and saw a very beautiful girl turn toward the dock. When she saw Jack, Brittany removed her sunglasses to squint the distance between them. Suddenly, she lifted a hand to her lips, and blew a kiss good-bye.

Margie winced. With what little she knew about Jack Ivan, she couldn't imagine he would take such rejection lightly.

"I'm going to kill her," he spit out, confirming Margie's suspicions. "I'm going to choke her until she turns blue."

Margie thought of losing herself in the crowd. Maybe she could slink back toward her car, hopefully unnoticed by the bloodthirsty Jack Ivan.

Not nearly quick enough. She offered a feeble grin

when Jack caught her elbow to spin her around to face him. "Come on. Let's find out where the next port of call . . ."

"Miami," she interrupted, trying to cut their relationship quickly.

He eyed her suspiciously. "How do you know?"

"I've sailed on cruise ships before and the boat always docks in Miami."

"Good," Jack responded. "Drive me there."

Margie eyed him like she would a mutant growth in a Tupperware bowl. "Absolutely not." She tried to walk around him.

Jack stepped in front of her. He still had her by the elbow and his dark eyes considered her face and hair. "I really need you to help me, Margie. It's too much to explain right now, but I've got to stop Brittany from marrying Andrew McDonald."

"Jack," she expressed patiently. "You've got to learn when a relationship is over."

"*Nothing* is over."

Margie pointed at the ship. "She just gave you the big kiss-off."

"It doesn't matter," he insisted, shaking his head, then saying with resolve, "Drive me to Miami."

"I don't even know you."

Jack frowned. "What's to know? This isn't a date. We're just going for a drive."

"No, we're not."

"Yes, we are."

The ship's horn blared at the mouth of Tampa Bay.

Plainly, Jack thought he had wasted time arguing and switched to blackmail. "If you won't drive me to Miami then I'll call the police and my attorney concerning the damage done to my Jeep. I'm sure a lawyer can get a little jingle out of a girl who drives a hundred-thousand-dollar sports car."

Margie narrowed her eyes. "That's extortion."

"I'm a desperate man," he seethed and then released her arm to stand at his full height. "If you'll agree to drive me to Miami, then I will pound out the bumper of my Jeep with a hammer and we'll call everything equal." He waited for her answer with half-closed, sparkling eyes. "Five hours there and five hours back. Or, five million in damages."

Margie laughed at such boldness. "You know, Mr. Ivan, I thought you were mildly attractive when I first saw you."

He smiled at her confession and shrugged modestly, as though she spoke truth and not sarcasm.

"But I was wrong. You are a mean and ugly man."

Her assessment seemed to surprise him and he shifted his weight.

"You would blackmail me after all I've done for you?"

"What have you done for me besides get in my way?"

"I drove you here," she reminded him and walked toward her car. She pulled the keys from her purse.

Jack followed her. Coming around her left shoulder, he accused, "You only drove me because I threatened to take your car."

She stopped to stare at him. "Right." With puckered

brow, she declared, "I don't blame the girl for leaving you, Jack. Any woman in her right mind would leave you."

"You don't know anything about it."

"And I don't want to," she told him, walking around him. "I've got other things to do, you know? I need to find out the difference between Swiss and Italian butter-cream. My life cannot be put on hold just to drive you to Miami."

Jack trailed her, passed her, and reached the Jaguar first. He blocked the keyhole with his hand. "Margie— Margie," he cooed, trying to catch her eye. "You know I need your help."

She stopped trying to fit her key past his fingers. "I don't want to drive you anywhere, Jack. I don't like you."

He looked wounded. Grabbing his heart, he proclaimed, "That hurt." Then he straightened. "Okay, I'm over it." He still blocked her path. "So, have you made up your mind about driving me to Miami?"

"I just told you, *no.*"

Jack leaned closer and dropped his voice. "Then I'll see you in court."

She lifted her eyes and saw his intent. He seriously meant to sue her. Uncle Bonny would burst an artery if she had to seek legal help to keep five million dollars in the bank. Taking a deep breath, Margie spat out, "All right, all right, *all right.*"

Jack grinned, showing white teeth. His brown eyes glittered with victory. He moved toward the passenger side before she could change her mind.

Watching him, Margie pointed her keys in a threatening gesture. "Be warned, Jack. When we reach Miami, you can jump out of the car, because I won't slow down long enough for you to shut the door." She didn't care that he frowned disapprovingly at her outburst. If Jack thought she cared one whit about his curdling love affair with Brianna or Brittany or whatever the girl's name was, then he was sorely mistaken.

Tossing her purse onto the backseat, Margie reached for the cell phone lying on the console. She held it between her shoulder and chin while she dropped into the driver's seat.

The answering machine picked up on the third ring. Margie said, "Hey, it's me. I'm going to Miami for the evening. I have the cell phone if you need to reach me. Love you." Flipping the phone shut with one hand, she tossed it toward her purse, and then looked at Jack while she started the car. She shoved the stick in reverse but braked when she saw someone crossing behind the Jaguar. The man had a bushy mustache, and bushy hair that he had tried to sweep into a ponytail. It still puffed out at his ears, though.

Jack asked, "You've learned to look before backing out your car? It's a little late for that."

"Don't aggravate me while I'm driving," Margie told him, reversing and then shoving the stick into first gear. "I need to concentrate."

"Now you're concentrating?"

She tossed him a placid look. "What are you, a detective? Why do you ask so many annoying questions?"

Jack laughed and then sat back to get comfortable in the white leather seat. "No one has ever accused me of annoying them."

"That's amazing, really, that's unbelievable." When he didn't reply, Margie asked, "Well, what do you do for a living, besides stalk women?"

He never lost his derisive grin. "I'm a rancher."

Margie drove over railroad tracks on a road leading to Highway 41. "Jack Ivan the rancher," she tried on for size. "I've never seen a ranch in downtown Tampa."

"I live outside of Tampa. I only came to Brittany's office after she called to tell me her intentions."

"And when you discovered her gone, you rushed into the street and were nearly crushed by a Volvo."

Jack twisted around to look at her. "Where were you?"

"Just a stranger in the crowd," she told him, keeping her eyes on the road. "We all talked about you after you tore off. You were jaywalking . . . jay-running, actually."

"No kidding?"

"No kidding. I was standing next to the guy who hollered, 'Where's the fire?' "

Jack snorted a laugh. "I remember that."

Margie nodded. "If we were in a movie, he would've had the great line and I would have been standing right next to him. I could've been on the big screen. I coulda been somebody."

"I coulda been a contender," Jack rallied, recognizing the movie line she recited. "Instead of a bum, which is what I am, let's face it."

Margie grinned. "Pacino."

"Brando."

"It was Pacino. Hand me my cell phone and I'll prove it to you."

Jack reached into the backseat. "Who will you call?"

"I know people," she explained. "I know lots of people."

"Do you know Marlon Brando?"

"Someone better," she said and pushed a button on the phone pad. When Cat answered, Margie asked, "Who said, 'I could've been somebody. I coulda been a contender. . . .'? Who?" She switched the phone to the other ear. "All right, thanks." She rang off and shoved the phone between the seats. "*On the Waterfront* starred Marlon Brando." When Jack rose a brow in an *I told you so* expression, Margie stated, "Well, that's one for me."

"You said Pacino."

"Brando."

Jack turned in his seat. "You said Pacino."

"Why are you talking to me while I'm driving?"

He sat back again. "I'm stuck in a car with Lucille Ball."

"Hey, this was your big idea."

Chapter Two

They stopped at a Shell station off old Exit 29. While Jack pumped gas, Margie used the ladies' room. She found him five minutes later buying a hot dog in the mini-mart. He hadn't seen her walk toward him. When he did look up, he took a double take and then smiled at Margie. "Want one?"

"I'm vegetarian and I don't eat pig," she told him. Then she looked at the older man behind the counter. "Your ladies' room could use a good mopping. My sandals kept sticking to the floor."

The clerk replied by handing Jack his food.

Jack said, "You're in a gas station, not the Four Seasons."

"It smelled like wet dog in there."

He pulled his wallet from his hip pocket. "Do you want something to eat?"

Margie scanned the selections behind the glass case on the counter.

"Certainly not any of this." Then she asked the clerk, "Do you have veggie burgers or bee products of any sort?"

Jack snorted his disapproval. "Bee products?"

"If you want to die that way, die that way," she told him, frowning at his hot dog. "You'll never reach forty."

"And you'll never reach twenty-five the way you're going." He handed the clerk money for gas and food and then headed toward the door.

She didn't know what he meant by that last statement, so Margie followed Jack and asked him.

"You mean no one has ever had a major meltdown in your presence and made a grab at you?" He held the door open for her.

Margie thought about it on the sidewalk. "No, but my sister tried to strangle me once in the school lunch line. I think she was kidding."

"Maybe," Jack said with a mouthful of hot dog. He stepped toward the driver's side of the car.

Margie headed toward the passenger side, and then paused. "Hey, look," she said, nodding at a dark blue sedan. "Doesn't that guy look familiar?"

Jack's eyes followed her nod. "Who?"

"You don't see the fellow over there leaning on the car and looking at his cell phone?"

"I see him. So what?"

"So what is, I keep seeing him."

She tossed the keys to Jack and he caught them to his chest. "We're on a highway. You see the same people over and over." He finished his food in one last bite and climbed into the Jaguar.

Behind the wheel now, Jack drove fast. He tried to make up for the time spent buying gas by traveling 175 miles per hour—or so it seemed.

"You're speeding," Margie accused, holding onto the grip above the passenger-side door.

"I'm going the same speed as everyone else," he explained. "See the blue car behind us? He's keeping up." He adjusted the mirror. "I want to reach Miami before the ship docks."

"If you plow off the road, we won't get to Miami at all. We'll be like the teenager who drove off a cliff and no one found him for eight days." She thought for a moment. "Bears almost ate him."

"There are no cliffs in Florida," Jack reminded her, keeping the same speed. "And I've never seen a bear."

"Well, what about alligators?"

"What about them?"

Margie stared out the windshield and adjusted her seat belt. "There are about a hundred ways I don't want to die. Right at the top of the list is being eaten by an alligator."

"What are we talking about?" Jack took his eyes off the road to scowl at her.

A bottle in the middle of the road caught Margie's attention. "Watch out for the glass!"

Jack tried to miss it but the back tire nailed the soda

bottle full force. He handled the steering wheel beauti-
fully, but the Jaguar swerved violently, skidded in the
breakdown lane, and then glided into the grass.

Margie glared at Jack. "There, you see that?"

"What do I see?" he asked, opening his door. "It's a
blowout."

She scrambled out of the car. "Bad things happen
when you drive too fast." She stood beside him at the
trunk of the car. "Do you know it's possible to drive right
through the middle of a Laundromat and emerge out the
back exit with your car still in one piece? Of course you
then have to deal with someone else's boxers on your antenna. And try explaining that one to Uncle Bonny, who
wants to know why someone is suing you over their Fruit
of the Loom getting ripped out of their hands."

Jack blinked slowly at her.

"I'm just saying bad things can happen."

He opened the trunk and rummaged inside. Suddenly, he frowned at Margie. "Where's the spare tire?"

She bit the inside of her lip. "I didn't replace it yet."

"You didn't replace it?"

Didn't she already say that? Did he want it in writ-
ing?

Jack slammed the trunk and leaned against the car.
Margie could see the muscle on his jaw work as he fought
to keep his temper. "Where's the cell phone?"

Margie brightened. "Oh, good idea." Just when she
thought all was doomed, Jack remembered the obvious.
"You're very smart," she told him, grinning. When she
emerged from the backseat, she saw his incredulous ex-

pression. "What?" she asked, holding the phone out to him. "I saw you roll your eyes. Are you implying that you're smart and I'm not?" When he didn't answer, only held out his hand for the phone, Margie declared, "I'll have you know I'm remarkably clever. I have a gift for languages and mathematics."

"Yeah, fascinating."

She gasped and then challenged, "Well, what can you do?"

Jack held the phone to his ear. "I can call for a tow truck if you'll leave me alone for a minute."

"Well, la-dee-da," Margie mumbled and propped herself against the Jag to wait. She supposed she could stick out her thumb and hitch a ride to the nearest Tire Kingdom but most of the traffic was in the westbound lane. One blue car passed them heading east, but the driver of the sedan seemed to have trouble of his own because he pulled onto the shoulder too, about a half-mile up the road.

Jack flipped the phone shut. "It will be a half hour before the tow truck gets here." He gazed at the azure sky and the five o'clock sun. "It's getting late."

Margie glanced at her bangle wristwatch. "We can still make Miami by six or six-thirty."

Jack leaned against the car and crossed one boot over the other. He crossed his bare arms too, and Margie could see the swelled veins running along his toned biceps. His hair tossed in the light breeze and he kept his eyes cast toward the pavement. Jack looked very sad just then and she felt a rush of sympathy for him. He must truly love Brittany to pursue her with such passion. It's what caused him to act so cantankerously and Margie instantly forgave him for, well, kidnapping her, blackmailing her, and not acting interested in her happy chitchat.

Jack was a fiery man, and a determined man, and he wasn't afraid to go after what he wanted no matter what sort of fool it made him look like. A girl had to have a grudging respect for that.

And what about Tyler Bonaguide? Would he chase after Margie if she ran off with another man?

Well, Margie had, hadn't she?

And where was Tyler now? Lunching with supporters who financed his bid for governor, that's where. What would Tyler think if he knew Margie was with a cowboy who was dark, handsome, and powerfully built?

"What's wrong, Margie?" Jack asked, interrupting her thoughts.

Caught mooning, she covered with, "I'm sorry, what?"

"You're looking at me as though my ears slid down my neck." He watched her closely now with those dark brown eyes.

Thinking to cheer his broken heart, Margie spoke candidly. "I was just thinking you *are* an attractive man."

His brow lifted. "Really?"

"Yes, and life will go on for you if you miss Brittany's boat, Jack. Floods of women will fall at your feet when you're ready to start over."

Jack twisted to face her. "Including you?"

"Of course not, but other women will, just you wait and see."

He looked puzzled and then asked, "Are you coming on to me?"

"I would never . . ."

"I'm not complaining," he told her, straightening to his full height.

She shook her head in bewilderment. "I'm happily engaged, thank you, and I was not coming on to you."

"Engaged?"

"Yes."

Unexpectedly, Jack reached out and seized Margie's wrist. Dragging her toward him, he lifted her left hand toward the sun. Then he bent to examine the stone on her pinkie finger. "This is your engagement ring?"

She tried to pull her wrist away but Jack twisted around, tucked her arm beneath his, and squeezed effectively enough to keep her still. His big fingers manipulated the small stone.

"That is not my engagement ring," she exclaimed. "Don't you think it's on the wrong finger?" She pushed hard on his shoulder to free her arm.

"What I think," he answered, releasing her, and facing Margie again, "is that you're a funny little prude."

"Prude?"

"Yes, *prude*. You and your bee products and your," he waved his hand in the air, "*I-can't-use-this-bathroom-because-my-one-thousand-dollar-sandals-stick-to-the-floor* attitude."

Well, he was just crazy. She would never pay a

thousand dollars for shoes—unless she really needed them for a special occasion. And this occasion was turning out to be nothing special!

Jack leaned against the car again. "So who are you engaged to anyway? Wally Cleaver?"

Margie cringed. Jack was nothing but sarcasm stuffed into blue jeans and a plaid shirt. "It's none of your business, did you know that? If I were you, I would worry about my own curdling romance."

Mocking concern crossed his tanned features. "Did you just use the word 'curdling'?"

"Yes, I did," she bantered stiffly and then ticked off, "Curdling, souring, and/or mildewing."

"Prude."

It took the mechanic little time to hook the Jag to his lift. Margie sat in the front seat of the truck wedged between Jack and the driver. Old newspapers filled the grimy cab. She moved the front page of the *Miami Sun* to sit.

"I use the paper to cover the holes in the leather," the driver told them while starting the engine. His name tag read Marcus Sanchez. Marcus explained, "This truck is nearly thirty years old and though the engine is holding up, the furniture isn't." He glanced at Margie. "I hope you don't get anything on the pretty outfit you're wearing. I usually don't have someone in the cab with me besides Buddy. Buddy is my bulldog."

Margie smiled and nodded and then eyed Jack with renewed annoyance. She blamed him for this predicament.

If he had driven slower, he would've seen the glass in the road, they wouldn't have had a blowout, and now she wouldn't be sitting on saliva-stained plastic, snagging her four-hundred-dollar pantsuit. Dog hair clung to the flared bottom of her pant leg.

It didn't take long for the service station attendant to plug and repair the tire while Margie and Jack waited in the snack shop. The entire process cost nearly fifty dollars. The attendant asked, "How long have you owned your car?"

"I don't know, three years, I think. Why?"

"You should let us check the battery. When I pulled the car around just now, the engine dragged when I started it."

"I'll wait, thanks," she told the man, aware of Jack's eagerness to get on the road again. The sun looked much lower in the sky when they stepped out of the service office. Dark clouds piled up in the east.

Margie still picked dog hair from her pantsuit. "Do you see any stains on my clothes?" She held out her hands so Jack could see the entire front of her suit and then she twirled for him to see the back of it.

"It all looks good to me, sweetheart," he told her before climbing into the passenger seat.

"Never mind," she snapped, sitting too. "I still smell like a dog, or is that you?"

He chuckled and sat back to get comfortable. "My scent is called wolf."

"Wolf?" Margie asked, starting the engine. "Then you smell like hot bologna at a picnic."

He ignored her last comment and slapped a rhythm on his thighs. "All right. Let's go, let's go. Quit picking hairs and let's go."

It took another forty-five minutes to reach Miami. Once there, Margie didn't know what to do or where to go. Jack consulted the map he had purchased at the service station. "You're on three ninety-five; turn off at the Biscayne Boulevard exit." He sat back, relaxed, with his elbow on the windowsill and his hand massaging his bottom lip. Suddenly, he sat up. "Get over into the left lane. You have to turn left."

"I can't get over. There's too much traffic."

"Be aggressive."

Margie swerved into the center lane while letting out a shriek about the same octave as the blasting horns around them.

"Pull over," Jack instructed. "Pull over now."

"I can't . . ."

"You missed it!"

She drove on for a minute until she could get into the right lane again and took the next exit off the interstate. "Turn here," Jack told her, clearly aggrieved by her performance behind the wheel. "We'll have to circle again and try to take the exit once more."

Margie saw a gas station, parked, and opened the driver's-side door.

"What are you doing?"

"You drive," she told him. "But don't wreck my car, Jack."

"Why not?" he asked while passing her at the trunk of the car. "You wrecked mine."

"Oh, forget it," she told him, turning around to head for the driver's side again. She tried to slide back into the bucket seat but Jack fought for it. She pushed forward until he grabbed her around the waist and pulled her out of the way.

Now he sat triumphantly in the driver's seat. "Hurry and get in," he called up to her. "We're running out of time."

Margie marched around the car and fell into the passenger seat. "Be careful."

He sat very close in the tight quarters. His white teeth flashed a smile. "I'm always careful, Margie. Now shut the door. This rocket is ready to burn."

Back on the highway, Jack missed the exit too. Margie grinned. "You missed it."

"Quiet!" he barked.

"I just thought you'd like to know."

He changed lanes swiftly to pull off the interstate again and then circled back for another try at it. A man in a yellow Volkswagen passed them on the left and made a crude hand signal at Jack.

"Well, that wasn't very nice," Margie responded. "Of course, you deserved it."

They drove past the service station where they had switched seats. "Hey, I recognize this place. What are we doing here?" She glanced at Jack. "Oh, that's right. You missed the exit."

"We won't this time," he informed her with a boldness that made Margie check her seat belt.

They were back on the highway again and approaching the exit. Horns blasted when Jack cut the Jaguar through traffic. Margie winced and crouched low in her seat as Jack violated several driving regulations. "That's how you do it," he told her, relaxing into his seat.

Red lights filled the car's interior.

Jack hit the steering wheel with the palm of his hand. "I cannot believe this," he mumbled peevishly as he maneuvered the car onto the shoulder of the road.

"What's so hard to believe?" she asked. "There are good reasons to obey speed and traffic laws." She flashed him a smile. "Now you're in for it."

He shifted to reach for the wallet in his hip pocket. "Will you knock it off?"

"It serves you right is all. Ever since I met you, you've been busting up the world in this mad pursuit of yours."

A police officer bent toward the window. His badge read *Nichols*. "When you're finished arguing, I'll need to see your license and vehicle registration." Margie popped open the glove box and handed Jack the white registration card.

"The car is hers," Jack explained.

Nichols bent to see Margie. "Stay in the car, please. I will return shortly." He walked toward his cruiser.

The traffic from the interstate sounded loud outside the car. Headlight beams struck at the mirrors and filled the darkening interior of the Jaguar. "I'm going to miss the ship, and then I'm going to murder you." Jack said this very offhandedly.

It was the third time he had referred to injuring the

innocent and Margie replied, "You know, slaughter is not the solution to every one of life's little problems, Jack." She sat further back in her seat. "And why is this my fault? You were the one driving like a madman."

"If you hadn't missed the exit in the first place, I wouldn't have had to drive like a madman. It's like you've cursed me."

Margie thought he might be surprised just how many times she *had* cursed him.

Street lamps came on and traffic looked like one long row of lights. Nichols returned to Jack's window and handed him three tickets to sign. "I'm citing you for reckless driving, speeding, and exiting the freeway improperly."

"Exiting the freeway improperly?"

"You drove over the median and took out a mile marker."

Jack signed the tickets and retrieved his license and the car registration. Once he rolled up the window, he stared at Margie. "Enough."

"Sorry," she offered between giggles. "Sorry." She straightened her face. Taking out a mile marker was serious business.

Jack took a quick right onto Port Boulevard. At the American Airlines Arena, he turned left and drove over the port bridge while watching for directional signs. Night settled and the enormous cruise ships looked like giant sea monsters beached in the harbor. Twinkling portal lights blinked in the darkness.

Locked gates kept them out of the parking lot. Jack pulled the car straight up to the fencing and honked the horn.

Margie grimaced. Why must he act so aggressively?

Jack honked the horn again.

"Will you stop? Obviously the lot is closed. You'll have to wait until morning to find Brittany."

"There's someone in the gatehouse."

"Yes," Margie agreed. "It's a guard, a guard with a gun. They shoot people with those things, you know, just for honking the horn."

Before she could continue the lecture, Jack opened the door and climbed out of the car to meet a uniformed guard at the fence. Margie could hear their conversation. Jack explained, "It's very important that I speak to someone aboard one of the ships. It's an emergency."

Margie rolled her eyes in the dark. An emergency?

"Is someone sick?" the guard asked. "Has someone died?"

Jack shifted his weight. "It's not that sort of emergency."

"The gates reopen at eight o'clock, sir. I'm sure you understand we have very strict security measures in place."

Sliding into the driver's seat, Jack let out a growl of frustration. The car's interior light went off when he slammed the door shut. "There has got to be a way past the gate."

"Why don't you try to call her?"

"Because she wouldn't answer, that's why. And if she did, she would hang up when she knew it was me."

"Send her a note."

"No," Jack firmly replied. "I've got to see her." He started the car's engine. "Tomorrow will be too late. Maybe it's already too late. People can marry while a ship is at sea, can't they?"

"I think so," she told him. Margie touched his arm, moved by his dismay. "But you're going to have to wait until morning, Jack. If you try to bust through a gate you'll wind up at Gitmo. Let's find you a hotel room. You and Brittany can sort this out in the morning."

He acted as if he hadn't heard her. Instead, he slowly drove past the fencing, as though looking for a hole to slip through.

Margie stopped trying to convince him with decent logic. "Why don't you just climb the wires?"

"Don't think I haven't considered it, but they're plugged in."

"You would be struck with high-powered voltage?"

It was just a question.

When Jack scowled at her, Margie recanted, "I-I'm kidding."

He heaved a sigh then. "You're right." Raking his hair back with one hand, Jack agreed. "I'll get a hotel room and come back first thing in the morning."

"Now you're being sensible."

It took them nearly an hour to find a hotel room. Most establishments were already booked full. Jack wanted a place within walking distance to the port. The Forty Winks Inn had one room available. The street-side building stood two stories high and had a giant blinking neon eye on top of the roof.

Margie shut off the car engine to walk to the door with Jack. She saw two full-size beds in the clean and comfortable-looking room. A dresser sat across from the beds and a vanity occupied the wall next to the bath-room.

"I guess this is good-bye, Jack," she told him at the door.

He nodded while poised with his hands on his faded jeans. The opened blue plaid sleeveless shirt revealed his muscled biceps and the ribbed tee beneath. The large golden crucifix flashed in the lamplight. After a long breath, he suggested, "You know, it's getting late. Why don't you find a hotel room and get some sleep?"

"Oh, no," she answered, "I'm fine."

He shook his head and walked toward her. "It will take five hours to get back to Tampa. It would put you home past two."

"I'm used to staying up late."

He stood right in front of her now. She had forgotten how broad he was and how tall until she had to crane her neck to look up at him. "The life of a socialite?" he asked in good humor. His dark eyes examined her face and then settled on her lips.

Margie took a slow breath to stop the tingling in her belly. What was she feeling? She had no business get-ting tingly over Jack Ivan. All day she had wanted nothing more than for this journey to end, but now faced with the prospect of saying good-bye, Margie paused.

He said, "The least I can do is buy you some dinner." He stuck the room key in his front pocket and led her out. "Come on, there's a steak place across the street."

Fortunately for Margie and Jack, the Ponderosa Steak House seated customers until nine o'clock. Margie passed on the steak and chose the pasta and greens from the salad bar. Jack ate steak and cheese fries.

Few patrons remained in the dining room. Margie and Jack sat beneath an antique saddle hanging on the wall. A Western theme dominated the décor, including the damaged wooden sign reading: DON'T RIDE YOUR HORSE INTO THE SALOON.

"You should feel right at home in here, Jack." When he looked up, she explained, "You being a cowboy and all."

"I'm not a cowboy," he told her. "I'm a cattleman."

Margie grinned at him while chewing a crouton. When she finished, she asked, "Where is your ranch; specifically, I mean?"

Jack cut into his steak. "Zephyrhills."

"Do you own a lot of property?"

"Three thousand acres."

"That's a lot of land." She selected another crouton with a good amount of cucumber dressing on it.

"My neighbor owns ten thousand."

Margie sat back. "Ten thousand? Well, he's set, isn't he?"

"You don't know much about ranching, do you?" When she shook her head, he explained, "There are ranches all over Florida with larger amounts of property than Andrew McDonald. They include prairies, pinewoods, and swamps, and parts of the Everglades. McDonald won't be set until he owns a lot more property than ten thousand acres." He cut another piece of steak but paused before putting it into his mouth. "What do you do, Margie?"

"What do I do?" She paused as well. "A job, you mean?"

"That's what I mean."

"I told you, I'm engaged."

He frowned at her. "That's not a job."

Obviously, he had never been engaged to Tyler Bonaguide. She told him, "It's what I'm concentrating on at the moment." She eased her back into the booth cushion. "It's a lot of work, you know, selecting the wedding clothes, deciding what length of gown to wear, finding the perfect location for the reception."

Tilting his head, Jack's eyes observed her left hand still resting on the table. "When are you getting married?"

"Soon," she offered. She picked at another crouton.

Jack stared at her with his fork dangling in mid-air while waiting for a more generous response.

Margie cleared her throat. "About a month."

"Yet you're only wearing a cheap pinkie ring. It looks like it came out of a bubble gum machine."

She righted the ring on her finger. "This did come out of a bubble gum machine."

"I would think a girl with your money could afford better jewelry."

Margie finished chewing. "This has sentimental value."

"Nothing else turns your finger so green?"

"I've had the pink glass reset into a gold band," she replied, leaning back in the booth again. "When I was a little girl, my nanny used to drag me and my sister along with her to the Quick Check store at Sunshine Plaza. While she stood in the checkout line, she would hand me a quarter to use at the prize machine."

Margie stared at her pasta and twirled it with her fork. "The first time I saw this ring, it was in the top of the glass bubble. Every week it sank lower and lower in the bowl. I knew it was mine and every week I would gaze into the machine to see if the pink-stone ring was still there. I concentrated really hard and recited, 'Ring of mine, pink in hue, bring me love that sticks like glue.'"

With a mouthful, Jack retorted, "You're kidding?"

"I was eight," she explained with a shrug. "One day I couldn't see the ring and was afraid it was gone. I just knew some other little girl bought it and would find love that stuck like glue." She sat forward to add intensity to the story. "But I put my quarter into the machine and recited my poem, and . . ."

He looked as if the story pained him to listen to it. "Yeah, what?"

She leaned back again. "Out pops a key chain with a miniature baseball bat on the end of it. I stood there simply devastated." She stopped twirling her fork and pointed it at Jack. "Then, all of a sudden, this boy came out of nowhere, put his quarter into the machine, and out came my ring."

Jack finished the story for her. "So you beat him up, took the ring, and ran off?"

Margie winced at his rendering. "No."

"Well, you're wearing it. What did you do?"

"What any girl would do in my place. I started to cry. He handed it over and took the key chain in return. He was so chivalrous that I've loved him ever since."

"You knew him?"

Margie blinked at Jack. "Well . . . no. But I vowed one day to marry him."

Jack snorted and finished chewing his steak. "Do you know how many boys have given up pink rings to girls at the bubble gum machine?"

She paused again. "Gee, I don't know."

"Any self-respecting boy would ditch such a girly prize. I did." He leaned his arms on the table. "I assume your fiancé did or you wouldn't marry him, right?"

"Right," she lied. She had never asked Tyler about it, but according to Jack many boys gave up pink rings at the bubble gum machine, so it was possible Tyler had as well. To take the focus off her own situation, Margie asked, "You gave up a ring at the bubble gum machine? That seems kind of sweet of you, Jack."

He lifted a shoulder as if it was no big deal. "She was bawling over it."

Could Jack be the boy who gave her the ring? No! Margie refused to believe it. It was too coincidental.

Finished with his plate of food, Jack pushed it away, leaned his elbows on the table, and rested his chin on his fist. "You never answered my question."

"What question?"

"Why aren't you wearing an engagement ring? Can't your fiancé afford one? Is he just a poor slob engaged to a rich girl?"

Margie wrinkled her nose. "Tyler is not poor. He gave me an engagement ring."

"Tyler?"

She leaned against the table, frustrated by his rapid-fire questions. "Tyler Bonaguide, if you must know."

"Bonaguide, Bonaguide," Jack thoughtfully replied while he wiped his mouth on a cloth napkin. Then he tossed it on his plate. "The bank manager?" He stared wide-eyed at her. "You're engaged to the bank manager?"

Margie's mouth dropped at the suggestion. "His son— I'm engaged to his son!"

"Oh, thank goodness. For a minute there I thought . . ." He grinned at the ceiling. "Tyler Bonaguide, hmm."

"Hmm, what?"

"I don't know, but the name conjures up the idea of a man who obeys traffic signals and speed limit laws."

She knew he meant to rile her but she couldn't quite hold back her defense. "I'll have you know Tyler has been ticketed on numerous occasions."

"You must be very proud."

"Of course I am."

"Because a man who can't break a rule now and then is half a man."

"Right."

Jack leaned closer. "And a woman who can't wear her engagement ring is half a woman." Still grinning, he stood and laid several bills on the table to tip the busboy. "Ready to go?"

Margie got to her feet. "There is a good reason why I'm not wearing my ring."

He returned his wallet to his hip pocket. "Hey, you don't have to defend yourself to me."

"I am not defending—" She stopped in mid-sentence when she realized how loud her voice sounded.

A busboy with bushy brown hair and mustache, wearing a green apron and paper hat, stared at her and then turned to collect the dirty dishes off another table.

Margie lowered her voice to hiss, "I am not defending myself. Tyler gave me a ring, a beautiful ring, a spectacular ring, and it's nothing a cattle poke like you would ever select. Yours would resemble a horseshoe or a cow patty."

Jack threw back his head and laughed uproariously.

Margie left him standing at the table.

A moment later he passed her on the left, twisted around, and hit the exit-door panel with his back. "I know what's wrong with you." He held the door and eyed her from his six-foot-three vantage while she walked out of the restaurant.

"There's nothing wrong with me."

In the lamplight she saw his bare biceps knot when he placed his hands on his hips. The cross around his neck was burnished bronze, just like Jack's features. He explained, "My uncle lived behind Sunshine Plaza when I was a kid. I used to spend Friday nights with him and my aunt."

Margie had no idea why he shared the information. "So?"

"So I'm the boy who gave you the bubble gum ring."

She knew he was teasing. "Right," she told him, stepping into the parking lot. The light breeze held the scent of rain.

Jack caught up with her again. "How sad that you swore you'd love me forever and now you're engaged to another man . . . a lesser man. And now you refuse to wear the engagement ring he gave you in favor of my small token of love."

"You had better stick to ranching, Jack. You have an awful sense of the romantic."

He closed his eyes with a grimace as though Margie had mortally wounded him. "I was going for tragic."

"Oh," she allowed. "Well, you achieved that."

All of a sudden, Jack grabbed her hand and when traffic allowed, he pulled Margie across the street.

"I may never cross with the light again," she told him, catching her breath on the next sidewalk.

"You're a bad girl at heart, I knew it." They'd reached the Jaguar and he opened the door for her. Jack watched Margie turn to face him. Her blue-green eyes sparkled in the lamplight and high color topped her cheekbones. He had spent nearly all day with the girl, and though he had thought her pretty, he had been too caught up in the race to find Brittany to pay attention to Margie. Now, he saw how trim and graceful she appeared in the sleeveless pantsuit that embraced the lines of her figure. Her skin was honey brown. White-blonde streaks coursed through the long layers of her golden hair, and Jack wondered what the texture would feel like against the rough calluses of his hands.

As if sensing his attraction to her, Margie moved to sit in the driver's seat. "Well, let's try to say good-bye again." She tugged on the door and then leaned away to slam it shut. Rolling down the window, she smiled up at him. "I have an inexpressible desire to rush home and get that ring back on my finger."

Jack nodded. He balanced one arm on the roof of the car and grinned down at Margie. "I'm sure Tyler Bonagoose will thank me for it."

"It's—it's Bonaguide."

He pretended confusion and frowned at her. "Bonaguide? Are you sure?"

She wrinkled her nose in an appealing way. "I'm pretty sure."

"Well, all right then, but I'm certain you said something about a goose." When she laughed softly, Jack boldly asked, "Are you certain you don't want to sleep over?"

Margie stared at him for a moment. Her shadowed eyes

seemed to analyze whether he meant what it sounded like he meant.

He meant it all right, but he wondered if she would take him up on the offer.

Breathlessly, she answered, "I need to get home."

He studied her mouth then and tried to imagine what it would feel like to kiss her. Leaning closer, he said, "Thanks for bringing me to Miami."

Flustered, she faced the wheel and turned the ignition.

A clicking sound came from beneath the hood. Margie gasped and stared at the dash. Twisting the key again, she heard the same buzzing sound. "The battery!" Pumping the gas pedal, she forgot all about Jack leaning down to kiss her.

Margie shoved the door open and swung her feet to the pavement. The maneuver made Jack jump out of the way. "It's the battery, isn't it?"

"Pop the hood," he told her, moving toward the front of the car.

"How do I pop the hood?"

He spun around to walk toward the driver's seat.

"I should've listened to that mechanic. He told me the battery sounded strange. What am I going to do now?"

"You're going to let me get into the car."

"Oh," she said, stepping toward the sidewalk.

Jack tried the engine again and then pulled the hood-release lever. Getting out of the seat, he explained, "I'll see if anyone has jumper cables in the office."

He came back ten minutes later without jumper

cables. "The clerk said there's a twenty-four hour Wal-Mart up the street. It's about a mile walk. You can stay here."

"I'll come with you," Margie told him, locking the door.

"I'll give you the key and you can stay in my room. Watch TV."

"I'd rather stay with you."

Tilting his head, he asked, "Can't get enough of me?"

"I've had plenty of you, thanks," she covered.

Chapter Three

Wihile Jack studied the car-maintenance supplies, Margie studied a pair of Capri pants and a sleeveless pink top. He found her forty-five minutes later still wandering through the clothing section. "Look at these cute pants." She held them up for him to see. "I've heard of Wal-Mart of course, but I've never shopped at one."

"You're kidding?"

"And look at this blouse that goes with it."

"I have bad news," Jack told her, instinctively fingering the fabric she held out. "They don't carry your battery."

"But they have my size in this blouse."

"You're not listening to me."

Margie stopped at the swimsuit rack. "I am. I was talking about clothes and you were talking about . . ." She frowned at him, trying to remember.

"Batteries."

"Right."

Jack looked into the shopping cart. "You'll have to come back in the morning to order your battery from the garage, or have the car towed to another service station."

Margie walked ahead of him. "That's fine," she answered after laying the pants in the cart. "I want to visit the shoe department before we leave." In wonderment she added, "Have you seen the cosmetics aisle?"

Margie's cell phone rang while she scouted the size 7 racks. "Cat?" She turned a corner and waved for Jack to follow her. "I'm tearing it up at Wal-Mart."

"Wal-Mart," Cat uttered. "I've heard about Wal-Mart."

"Why did you call?"

"The caterer wants to know if you want asparagus towers or broccoli on a plate with rillettes of salmon and caviar."

Margie stopped examining a pair of sandals to frown into space. "I don't know what you're talking about."

Cat shortened the question, "Broccoli or asparagus?"

Margie looked to Jack for help. "If you were a plate of salmon, what side dish would you choose? Broccoli or asparagus?"

He scowled at her. "If I were a salmon?"

"Oh, for heaven's sake," Margie interrupted. "What do you like better, broccoli or asparagus?"

"Broccoli."

"Who are you talking to?" Cat wanted to know.

"The average man," she answered, grinning at Jack.

"Well, ask the average man if he would like blueberry tart or banana leaf cones."

After Margie cupped the phone to her shoulder and asked, she came back with, "He said banana leaf cones. But he looks a little confused."

"I'm not confused," Jack complained.

Margie quieted him by raising a threatening finger.

Jack rolled his eyes.

"All right, that's settled," Cat continued. "Tyler is here. Do you want to talk to him?"

"Tell him I can't talk right now. I'll call him in the morning." Ringing off, Margie shoved the phone into her purse.

"Who can't you talk to, your fiancé?"

She ignored Jack to examine a pair of canvas mules. "My phone battery is low."

"Liar."

She held out the phone to show him. "I'm also roaming." She added the mules to her purchases.

He still rested his arms on the cart. "You didn't want Tyler to know you were with another man."

Margie shook her head. "I'm not with another man." Ready to go, she shifted to walk away. "I'm with you."

Jack pushed the cart again. "Ahh, the words every man longs to hear."

"You know what I mean," she tossed over her shoulder. "You're happily chasing Brittany and I'm . . ."

"Yes, but Brittany . . ."

". . . happily engaged."

Jack pulled the cart to a halt. "Are you?"

"Am I what?" she asked, smelling a candle in the box display in the middle of the aisle. She looked at the package. "Hawaiian Breezes."

Jack removed the candle from beneath her nose and placed it into the display box. "Are you happily engaged?"

"Of course. Why?"

He smiled as he considered her hair. There were tiny laugh lines around his eyes. "Well, you were sure quick to run off with me without considering your boyfriend."

Margie shook her head and walked toward the center aisle of the store. "I did consider Tyler. Actually, he is the reason I helped you."

"Tyler is the reason you helped me? That doesn't make sense."

"It doesn't have to make sense," she pointed out. "You and I are not engaged."

Jack jerked the cart to a stop again. "Then I want my ring back." He looked very serious standing there next to the granola bar display. His full mouth held no hint of a smile. His thick arms flexed hard as he held on to the cart.

"I will give the ring back to you when you return my key chain." Margie reached past him to select a box of oat bars. "Where is it?"

"Where is what?"

"The key chain."

He answered, "I keep it under lock and key in my study at home. I recite a poem over it every morning after I take it out of a heart-shaped box."

"I'm glad you're taking it seriously," she told him and walked toward the registers. They stood in the checkout line when reality struck. "Where am I going to sleep?"

Jack selected a Milky Way from the candy display. "I'll share my room." Margie frowned at him. "I don't think so," she told him, leaving no doubt she wasn't interested in anything more than getting some sleep. "There has got to be another room available."

"The desk clerk told the guy behind me that mine was the only room left in town. There's some sort of convention going on." He grinned at her. "Looks like you're stuck with me for a little while longer."

Margie handed her clothing to the cashier. "I am not sharing a room with you, Jack Ivan."

So, she shared a room with Jack Ivan. Somewhere Margie's life had taken a tragic turn! There she sat on the edge of the bed nearest the door while Jack lay comfortably on his own bed watching a rerun of *The Beverly Hillbillies.* Margie bit her thumbnail and then made herself stop. She never bit her nails.

"Will you relax?" He had his hands behind his head on the pillow. Still fully dressed, Jack crossed one boot on top of the other and didn't take his eyes from the sitcom. In the low light, the television's flicker caused his handsome features to turn shadowy and blurry and pink sometimes.

Margie pulled her thumbnail out of her mouth to say, "I am relaxed."

"You're as rigid as a two-by-four. Kick off your shoes and get comfortable."

She didn't know how Jack knew she sat rigid as a two-by-four. He wasn't even looking at her, unless he sneaked peeks at her when she wasn't sneaking peeks at him. Now Margie bit her lip.

Jack didn't miss the action. "If anyone has the right to be nervous, it's me."

"What do you mean?"

He swung his legs off the bed and dropped his boots onto the beige carpet. "I'm scared to fall asleep. I don't know what you'll do next."

"Why, because I chased the cabdriver down to get my last package from his backseat?"

"No, because you jumped on the cab and beat on the back window to catch the man's attention."

He exaggerated. The cab had barely pulled away from the curb when Margie rapped on the side of the car. Still, she liked his version best. "My new sneakers were in that bag." She turned to face him. "Besides, I would've never known what a fine sportsperson you are. How breathtaking to watch you dive into the opened car door."

Jack grabbed his chest in mock salute and sat up straight. "I am your trusted warrior." He stood and then leaned down to look Margie square in the face. "Honest, brave, and completely uninterested in you."

Margie furrowed her brow in indignation and her eyes scanned his features with displeasure.

She opened her mouth to argue, but Jack spoke over

her. "I, on the other hand, know that you find me attractive because you already admitted it."

She gave him a look of kindness. "I felt sorry for you when I said that."

"Right," he added smugly.

She got to her feet and Jack took a step backward. "I still feel sorry for you."

He didn't move when she tried to brush past him. "Now, listen," he began. "I'm going to take a shower, and I will lock the door if I must."

"You can trust me, Jack. I won't burst in on you."

"All right, good. I'm glad that's settled." He moved away to grab a towel from the vanity. With a last warning glance at Margie, he entered the bathroom and shut the door. She waited to hear him twist the lock. When he didn't, Margie smiled at his ludicrous act. He had put her completely at ease—by denying her attractiveness!

She stomped toward the mirror and then gasped at her reflection. Well, if she didn't look like a weed in the wind: flyaway hair and no makeup and worn-out mascara smudged beneath her eyes. See what traveling with Jack did to a girl?

After plugging in her cell phone, she brushed out her hair and washed her face. Jack hollered a foul word when she turned on the cold water faucet. It served him right. For meanness, she turned on the water again, just to hear him yell. That's what he got for calling her unattractive.

Jack came out of the bathroom toweling his dark

hair. He only wore jeans. Black chest hair glistened and formed a T down his belly. "Why did you do that?"

Margie pretended to watch *Bewitched* on the television set. "I'm sure I don't know what you mean."

"I'm sure you do." He sounded irritated and Margie looked at him. Water droplets balanced on his tanned and very broad shoulders. Watching her watch him, Jack let his towel drop and then lifted it again to cover his chest. "Do you mind?"

She ignored his protests and grabbed a granola bar. Opening the package, she pinched off a section, and delicately crunched the oats.

Jack came around to sit on his own bed. "So, you're good at number crunching, is that right?"

Margie frowned, trying to understand what he meant. Then she remembered their conversation on the roadside while they waited for the tow truck. "I said I have a gift for mathematics." She pinched off another bit of the snack bar.

"A gift, right." He sat back on the bed as before with his bare feet stretched out in front of him. "How gifted are you?"

She remembered he had lost his accountant today. "I studied syllogism and the doctrine of inference at Harvard."

"You went to Harvard?"

"Why are you asking? Do you need someone to look after the books on that ranch of yours?"

His eyes studied the television set again and he answered without looking at her. "No, I need someone to look after my affairs for me, and not just the money. I need someone who knows the law. Are you gifted in law too?"

"My fiancé is a lawyer, Jack. He's the president of the Bonaguide Law Association."

Jack whipped around to face her. "The banker's son is that joker on the television commercial?"

"That's Tyler," Margie said, nodding and smiling. Then she realized what he'd said. "He is not a joker."

His voice held a bit of wonderment when he repeated, "Your fiancé is the lawyer on TV." He sat up on the edge of his bed now and stared at Margie. "Well, congratulations to you." He grinned broadly and placed both elbows on his knees.

Suspicious, she threw him a careful look. "What do you mean?"

Jack chuckled. "I mean congratulations. Isn't he running for councilman or something?"

"Governor."

He stared at the ceiling. "He's perfect for you: well dressed, law-abiding, and unexciting."

"He is not."

Jack sat back on the bed again and crossed his feet at the ankles. "Sure he is. He wears three-piece Armani suits."

"I meant—"

"And he'd better stay law-abiding if he hopes to get elected."

Margie sat up now. "Tyler is very exciting!"

Grimacing, Jack declared, "Did I need to know that?"

"You are contemptible," Margie exclaimed, snatching a pillow behind her and throwing it at him.

He captured the pillow mid-air and stuffed it behind his head. "I try my hardest." He didn't pursue the subject further and patted the front of his jeans.

"Do you have any change? I want to buy a soda."

Margie dragged her purse toward her and then pulled out the wallet to hand him a dollar in change. "You're not going out like that are you?"

"Like what?" His dark hair matted on his powerful chest and hard-muscled abdomen. Smirking at her, because he seemed to know exactly what she thought, Jack flexed his big biceps and teased, "You want me to cover my guns?"

"I'm referring to the fact that you don't have your boots on."

Jack stared at his feet.

Standing, Margie reached for his plaid shirt hanging across the chair. She handed it to him and said, "I think I'll come with you."

"I'll bring you a drink. What do you want?"

"I don't know. That's why I want to come with you, to see the selection."

She grabbed her purse and then walked out the door behind Jack.

"I'll tell you right now they don't have bug sap or anything else you want to gulp down made from bees."

She smiled at him. "That's what I like about you, Jack. You use all the academic terms."

The dark sky opened up and rain poured down outside the narrow overhang. They were on the second floor and took the flight of steps to the bottom level, where an ice machine vibrated against the wall in the stairwell.

Jack studied the soda selection. It started to rain harder and Margie slipped beneath the stairs to find shelter from the blowing rain. "Buy me a grape soda," she told him from her covered spot.

He glared at her through the sweeping rain. His pant legs were wet and his feet looked nearly underwater. "Get over here."

"I don't want to get wet," she shouted over the downpour.

Jack shook his damp hair. "I told you to stay in the room."

Margie handed him a dollar bill that was drenched before it hit his hand.

"This won't work, give me some quarters."

Margie dug in her purse for more change.

"Come on, come on," Jack rushed her. "I'm starting to drown."

"I can't see. It's too dark."

"Forget it then. You can share with me."

"I want grape." She found a quarter and a dime and held them up for him to see.

"Thank you. Now I can buy a newspaper."

Margie slumped against the wall. "That was for my soda."

"It's not enough. Besides, I want to see the sports section." After grabbing a paper, Jack took Margie's arm and led her toward the stairs. He dragged her along behind him beneath the overhang. Her powder-blue pant-suit started to turn a deep-blue shade from the rain.

Thunder crashed and lightning streaked toward the earth. Margie did a rapid shuffle to stay close to him. When they reached the door, Jack pushed but it didn't open. He twisted around to frown at Margie. His features lit up with another flash of lightning. "Did you lock the door?"

Margie had to yell over the thunder. "Of course I locked the door."

"Did you grab the key off the dresser?"

"I thought you had the key." She wiped rain off her face and pushed a loose tendril from her forehead. "Why didn't you bring the key?"

"Because *I didn't lock the door.*" He dropped his hand from her arm and gazed across the parking area toward the office. Sheets of rain blew crossways on the pavement, turning the potholes into pools of mud that shimmered in the street lamps. "I'll run over to the office."

"But, the lightning . . ."

"The storm is passing," he said, dropping his paper by the door and marching toward the stairs. He stopped when an explosion of wind blew rain that hit him like a dump truck full of ice.

Margie tried to duck behind him.

Jack turned on her. "What are you doing? Stay here." Water dripped off his straight nose and he wiped his mouth hard with the side of his hand.

"I'm not staying in a hallway where a giant eyeball winks at me. It reminds me of the movie *It.*"

"It what?"

"Just *It*."

"What's 'it'?"

For crying out loud!

"Are we going?" Margie asked him and then dashed into the rain after him when Jack sprinted into the parking lot.

According to the Weather Channel, Florida was the lightning capital of America. Margie had never paid much attention to that fact until a sizable blast of the stuff went off when she and Jack were somewhere in the middle of the parking lot. Streaks of fire streamed about and parked cars lit up like neon signs in Vegas. High voltage seared the air. Then it was dark again, darker than anything Margie had ever experienced before. She didn't know which way to run and slammed headlong into Jack, who was running back toward the overhang.

When the next bolt flashed, his face jumped right into hers and he mouthed something, but Margie only caught the word *lightning*.

Another shaft of light smacked the parking lot and Jack and Margie grabbed hold of each other and started running. When it was all over and they were safely beneath the office's overhang, Margie was sprawled spread-eagle on the sidewalk and Jack wore one of her spike-heeled sandals on his ear.

"Where's the other one?" she questioned when he dropped the shoe on her stomach.

"I don't know, let me check." He searched his hair,

the front of his shirt, and the back pocket of his jeans—
or some place thereabout. Then his mouth dropped open
like he'd found her footwear in a place it was never
meant to be stuck.

Rolling to her knees, she pushed to her feet. "Forget
it," she told him.

Jack slapped open the glass door of the small office
and dripped his way to the counter. "I'm locked out of
my room," he explained. Rain turned his long hair
nearly black and he pushed the wet mop out of his face.
"I need another key for two-oh-nine."

"We all need something, don't we?" the man answered. He was a lean-jawed man with stooped shoulders. "That will be twenty dollars."

Jack frowned. "How much?"

"Twenty dollars."

"I didn't lose my key. I left it in the room."

Margie went through her purse for her wallet. "We'll
take it."

"No, we won't," Jack told her. "I'm not paying
twenty bucks for a key when I'll return it in five minutes."

"You can return the key in two minutes but you'll pay
to get it in the first place," the clerk told him.

Jack apparently meant to stare the man down while
dripping all over his counter.

"Take the money," Margie offered, holding out a
twenty-dollar bill.

A stingy smirk touched the man's stubbly face.
"Room two-oh-nine, right? You only paid for a single

unit," he reminded Jack. "You didn't say you would be sharing the room." His buggy eyes slipped over Margie's wet pantsuit.

Jack tried to explain. "Her car won't start."

"What you're saying is you've abandoned a vehicle in my parking lot?" The clerk pulled a registration book from beneath the counter. "Double occupancy will cost you another forty-four-fifty. Towing the vehicle will cost sixty-nine."

So, he wasn't just a one-trick guy.

Margie asked, "How about I give you sixty-nine not to tow the vehicle?"

"Sounds reasonable to me," he said, poking at a dirty calculator, and then started over when a button stuck.

"One thirty-three fifty," Margie told him, since she didn't want to grow old while he labored over the math.

Jack's dark eyes rounded on her. "Quiet," he insisted. "We'll pay the twenty."

"I'll take the hundred and fifty three."

"Visa?" Margie offered.

"Cash."

She shook her head. "I only have two hundreds."

"I'll take it."

Margie looked for her shoe on the way back across the parking lot. Only light rain drizzled now and sprinkled the potholes. The lightning had moved on toward the west and she could still see the hint of it in the distance. "I feel like the last rose of summer," she grumbled, climbing the stairs behind Jack and holding her orphaned sandal.

He stopped to pick up the newspaper and then stuffed it beneath his armpit. "Do you ever stop complaining? Is it me?" He stuck the key in the lock but it jammed halfway because he was impatient and twisted too hard. He yanked and then yanked again until he was as mad as fire. That's when the newspaper popped out from beneath his arm and shot over the railing. All the sections fluttered in the breeze, mixed with the drizzle, and then landed on top of a dark blue sedan parked next to the Jaguar.

"Let me," Margie told him, taking over the job. When the door opened, Jack marched to his side of the room and ignored Margie and she ignored him. Neither of them spoke the rest of the night and after she fell asleep, Jack switched off the television set.

Chapter Four

Margie woke when the door slammed shut. Jack ripped open the draperies and rosy sunlight streamed into the room. She sat up in bed and grabbed the covers for defense. Not understanding why Jack acted so angry, she asked, "What's wrong?"

"I'll tell you what's wrong. Brittany's ship did not dock in Miami last night. It docked in Nassau." He stood beside the bed with his hands on his hips. His dark eyes burned in fury.

"Oh."

Jack leaned toward her as she sank deeper into the propped-up pillows. "'Oh'? That's all you have to say? Do you know where Nassau is located?" His fists rested on the blanket now as he balanced himself menacingly above her head.

"It's in . . ."

"That's right, it's not in Miami. You said you had been on cruises before and the boat always docks in Miami."

"I—I might have been mistaken."

"Oh, you think?"

The man in the next room pounded on the wall near Margie's head. "Shut up in there!" his voice charged through the wall.

"You shut up!" Jack hollered in response.

Margie began to scoot toward the other side of the bed.

Jack grabbed her by the arm. "You dragged me all the way down here. . . ."

Facing him bravely, Margie tried to pry his large fingers from her upper arm. "I did not drag you anywhere."

"I didn't need to come to Miami. I could've taken a plane out of Tampa yesterday and this whole mess would've been settled last night—in *Nassau.*" He snatched her hand to stop her prying fingers.

Margie's feet still worked their way off the bed and she began to deflate into a sea of bed blankets. Yet his last phrase made her pause and she scooted upward again. "What did you say about a plane?"

Her question seemed to throw Jack. "I could've taken one out of Tampa?"

"That's it."

He studied her with a bit of caution now. "What's it?"

Margie, already out of bed, headed for the bathroom to shower and change. She turned around once to cast him a happy face. "I have a pilot's license."

"No . . . no, Margie, forget it."

* * *

They didn't fly out of Miami until almost ten-thirty because of air traffic and because Jack still tried to book a commercial flight. When he realized the fastest way to get to the Bahamas was to let Margie fly them, he rented a Cessna twin engine craft.

At eleven o'clock, she removed her headset to grin at Jack. "Look to your right. Is that a cruise ship? Maybe it's Brittany's boat."

"Just keep your eyes on the road."

Margie frowned. Did he just tell her to keep her eyes on the road? "Are you afraid to fly?"

"I'm afraid of you."

He didn't look too good. His usual healthy features took on an ashen shade and sweat beaded on his upper lip. Margie turned to check the instrument panel and took the small plane to twenty-five thousand feet. Glancing at Jack again she asked, "So, you're okay? Everything is running smoothly. I'm sorry there's no stewardess to take your drink order."

"I'm sorry there's no bridge to the Bahamas."

"Someone should've built one of those long ago." She checked the airspeed. "Don't be nervous, Jack. I'm an experienced pilot."

He leaned back in an obvious attempt to relax. "When did you learn to fly?"

"I had to write a school report on Amelia Earhart."

"The woman they never found?"

Margie nodded, eyeing his troubled features. "Because I had to write the report, I became interested in flying. I imagined a life of freedom where I didn't answer to anyone," she said dreamily. "My father took me to flight school and I received a pilot's license before I received my driver's license." She patted his hand. "Don't you worry, Jack. I'll have you in the Bahamas by eleven-thirty."

The bright sunshine winked off the plane's cowl as it hummed along smoothly. Rolling waves welcomed visitors to the Devil's Triangle. In the distance, Margie could see the first of the graceful constellation of islands arcing away from the south coast of Florida.

Suddenly, a chime went off. Jack looked at her in surprise as though he thought it was some sort of warning buzzer.

Margie reached for her purse. "Cell phone," she explained and smiled at him.

"Can you do that?" Jack asked, sitting stiffly again.

"What?"

"No cell phones on an airplane. I know that. Everyone knows that."

"Everyone believes that," she said him, leaning toward him. "But it's not true. Airlines just want you to use the phone on their plane."

"I don't care. I just don't want to crash. Keep your hands on the wheel."

She shrugged. "Do you want to steer while I take this call?"

"*No.*"

Margie handed him the phone and he mashed a button to greet the caller. Then he said, "No, you don't have the wrong number, she's right here." He handed her the phone and stared out the window.

Thinking it was her sister, Margie plugged the phone into the dash to take the call on speaker. She announced, "Italian."

Tyler's voice filled the cockpit. "What?"

Margie's eyes widened and she glanced at Jack.

He smiled but didn't look at her.

"Hey there, Tyler," she acknowledged smoothly. "I thought you were Cat."

"What about Italians?"

"Italian buttercream," she told him, as if that might explain something.

"Are you speaking in code?"

Jack looked at her and chuckled softly.

"No, just trying to choose the icing for our wedding cake, darling. What are you doing?"

"You're at the bakery," Tyler assumed, and his voice sounded easier with the statement.

Sticking to the flow of conversation, Margie asked, "What would you like, Italian or Swiss buttercream?"

Tyler's voice cracked over the connection in the plane. "Margie, I've left the details to you. Please handle these things by yourself. You know how busy I am right now."

Margie waited patiently while Tyler said his piece and smiled at Jack. "I will handle everything," she told Tyler and then asked, "What was it you wanted?"

"Dinner."

"It's only eleven-fifteen," she answered brightly.

Tyler hesitated and then said, "Tonight . . . dinner tonight, what are your plans?"

"To drive back to Tampa."

"From where?"

"Miami."

"You can buy a perfectly good wedding cake in Tampa, Margie."

"It never hurts to see what options we have."

"Since you're not going to be home, I guess I'll go to dinner with Machen by myself. He wants to discuss the victory celebration."

"Mmm, sounds like fun."

"What?"

Margie raised her voice and leaned toward the speaker. "I said it sounds like fun."

"Where are you, in a vacuum cleaner?" asked Tyler.

"This is a very bad connection."

"Will I see you tomorrow?"

"Definitely. You will definitely see me tomorrow."

Tyler said good-bye and Margie unhooked the phone.

Jack scrunched his brows, as if he was very confused about something. His dark eyes glittered in the bright light of late morning. "Why didn't you tell Tyler you were flying me to the Bahamas?"

"Well, why do you think, Jack? Some things are better explained in person." She shoved her phone into her purse again. "What was I supposed to say? We're chasing after Brittany so Jack can stop the wedding because he was too stupid to tell her—"

The plane did a lurching roll toward the left and Margie stopped chatting to study the instrument panel.

Jack sat straight in his seat. "What's wrong?"

"We seem to have lost some fuel."

"How did we do that?"

Margie shrugged. " 'Some' is a comparative term, Jack."

"You're saying you didn't check the fuel gauge before we left the airport?"

His skepticism was getting on her nerves. "Of course I checked the gauge. There's a leak somewhere, that's all. Fortunately, there's a reserve tank of fuel on the plane. Unfortunately, you're going to have to climb out and hang on to something to pour it into the tank."

Oh, for heaven's sake, of course she's kidding.

"I'm joking," she mollified. "All I have to do is flip a switch." She turned the dial to the reserve tank position. "However, I didn't check the fuel in the reserve tank."

"Are you still joking around?"

Margie shook her head. Her mouth went dry and her stomach tingled.

"Why didn't the plane warn us? Isn't there some warning device on this thing?"

"Um, there's supposed to be. It's possible that there is something wrong with the electronics. . . ."

"Your cell phone!"

"This has nothing to do with my cell phone," she countered calmly.

"Whatever, I don't care. Just tell me what we're going to do. Are we turning back to Miami?"

"No, we're not going to turn back." She gazed at him in a kindly manner. "We're going to set the plane down near one of those barrier islands."

"We're going to *crash?*"

Really, Jack Ivan was turning out to be a poor traveling companion. He didn't grasp the idea that there were always mishaps when flying abroad. Margie explained, "We'll land near shore and swim to the island." She thought a moment. "You do know how to swim, don't you?"

Jack gave his typical response. "*Yes, I know how to swim!*"

"Stop yelling at me." She took a careful and deep breath and then thought of a way to keep him busy. "Turn the dial there to channel one twenty-one point five. Someone will ask for the plane's call numbers. They're right on the dash. Tell them we're calling in a Mayday."

"I'm calling in a Mayday," Jack responded in stupefaction. "Are you sure you're not kidding around?"

"*Yes, I'm sure I'm not kidding around.*"

Jack stared at her like she had lost her mind. Then he reached for the radio mic and made the call.

Margie reduced the power and moved the throttle toward her. They were still two thousand feet above the water. She leveled the nose and explored the ocean. "We need calm water to land."

Jack replaced the hand-held into the holder. "We're over the Atlantic Ocean. There is no calm water."

"Then we'll find the headwind." She reduced the

power again. With so little fuel, the engine began to sputter and Margie moved the nose of the craft to five degrees above the horizon. "I'll have to do a nose-up landing to keep the propeller out of the water." She grinned at Jack. "We don't want to flip end-over-end, do we?"

Jack hung onto the grip above the door again. He stared at the waves beneath them coming closer and closer. "No, we don't want to do that." At ten feet above the water, Margie pulled back on the yoke. "Get ready to open your door. Wait until the plane hits once and then kick it open."

"How many times are you planning to hit?"

Squeezing the saltwater from her ponytail, Margie sat on her heels and dumped the contents of her purse onto a large rock. The cosmetics were in waterproof packages but the tissues looked limp. Margie laid her financial report on the boulder to dry in the sun. The ink hadn't run, and if the papers dried properly, she could still use them.

Jack stared at the ocean and at the Cessna staggering in the waves. One of its wings dipped beneath the water. Margie approached him and then sat in the sand. "We should make a garland; the plane is dead." She had changed into her newly purchased black and wild–pink flowered capri pants and sleeveless blouse before they left the hotel. With her legs stretched out in front of her, she tapped the white sneakers together to loosen the sticky sand.

Jack eyed Margie. His sooty lashes still held little droplets of water so that they stuck together. He had removed his shirt and sat in the sand in his jeans and wet ribbed T-shirt. "You've cured my fear of flying." Tilting his head, he admitted, "I simply don't care anymore."

"That's the spirit," she told him, proud of his good sportsmanship. She bent her knees to her chest and then clasped her arms around them. "It's really quite lovely out here." Jack didn't respond, so Margie asked, "Don't you think so?"

"What I think is that we're marooned."

"Well, if we are, you won't have to pay those three traffic tickets in Miami." She smiled at him. He didn't return the expression. Before he could get too cranky, Margie reminded him, "When you called in the Mayday, you gave them our position. The Cessna has an emergency signaling device onboard and it's broadcasting our location right now. Don't you worry, Jack, the Coast Guard is on the way."

"That sounds familiar to me," he said, appearing quite calm as he watched the bobbing plane in the dazzling blue ocean. "It sounds like, 'The ship always docks in Miami.'" Now he stared hard at Margie. "That's what it sounds like to me. Where's the cell phone?"

She reached for the wet telephone. "Who do you think you're going to call?"

"Nine-one-one."

"I just told you, the Cessna is broadcasting our position."

Jack turned away from her to hold the phone to his ear.

Margie got to her feet and walked to the water's edge, staying out of the lapping waves. Other small islands dotted the horizon. The clear blue water twinkled in the late morning sunshine. She had seen views like this before while visiting the islands. They could be at a posh and exclusive resort—if they weren't stranded.

"We're near Andros Island," Margie called over her shoulder. When Jack didn't answer, she turned around again. "Unless we're closer to Cuba than I thought."

"We're not anywhere near Cuba," Jack maintained, dismissing her concern.

"Well, when Fidel Castro answers the phone, don't tell him I'm with you." She picked up a colorful shell to examine and then paused. "Wait a minute. We're in the Bermuda Triangle."

Jack shook the phone and replaced it to his ear. "It's not working. I keep getting a beeping signal."

"That's right. In the Triangle, all instrumentation goes out of whack. Maybe we weren't really out of fuel. Maybe the plane's panel reacted to some bipolar pull in the atmosphere." Nodding, she came to sit in front of Jack again. She leaned back on her heels and placed her palms on her thighs. "It could be part of that whole parallel universe thing."

Jack raised a brow. "Is that your excuse for running out of gas?"

Margie gaped at him. "There was a leak . . . and

aren't you forgetting I'm the one who safely landed the plane? Stop pointing fingers, Jack. I saved your life."

"Saved my life?" He got to his feet and shoved the phone at her. "You endangered my life." His dark brown eyes scorched her features. "I knew it too. I knew the moment I strapped on the seat belt that my days were numbered."

"You didn't have to board the plane."

Jack's eyes narrowed and he leaned down and toward Margie. "I'm talking about when I got into your car."

He was just too mean and too stubborn to argue with, so Margie got to her feet and spun away from him. She marched toward the boulder where she had laid out her papers. They hadn't dried yet, so she scooted them aside, dropped a rock on them to hold them in place, and then sat on the boulder with her knees up.

Jack watched the horizon for a ship.

The Bahamas by eleven-thirty was looking iffy.

An hour and a half later, Jack still stared at the ocean and Margie wrinkled her nose at him. How could he sit in one place for so long? Maybe he hit his head when she landed the plane.

Well, she wasn't going to stand idly by and not build a shelter. She imagined surviving in high fashion, like Ginger Grant did on *Gilligan's Island.* She would need to build a hut though, and she wasn't sure where she would find a long silk gown.

She sat in the sand next to Jack to see what the attraction was; nope, she didn't see that it made one bit of difference in their circumstance. It was picturesque however, with the small breakers hitting the shoreline. Seaward, the white caps gave way to emerald green and then to a pale shade of ice blue. A tropical breeze rustled the palms and palmettos behind them.

"I've never been to the islands," Jack admitted, without turning toward her. Margie smiled at him. Perhaps the scenery relaxed him. Perhaps he could forget, for just a little while, that he was in hot pursuit of Brittany. She said, "Have you never been off that ranch of yours?"

"Sure I have, but I traveled north mostly and out west once. I'm not the roving socialite you are."

She grinned at his idea of her life. "My travels these days are limited to the colleges I attend."

"How many colleges is that exactly?" He turned his head to look at her with those very brown eyes. The long layers of his hair lifted in the breeze.

"Exactly?"

"You should be able to count them, Margie."

"All right, all right, let me think," she told him, facing the stalled plane bobbing out in the water. "My first year, I went to Harvard, but I already told you that."

"Mathematics, right?"

"Right. The next year I went to Liberty because of their arts program. I went to Cedarville for a while and then to Yale."

"You changed your major?"

She picked up a small shell. "Something like that. I

went to the University of California for a semester and to U.S.F., and, oh, I went to Princeton. How many does that make?"

"Seven."

"Yes, seven."

"That's ridiculous."

"You sound like Uncle Bonny."

Jack frowned at her. "Who is Uncle Bonny?"

She leaned toward him. "Morris Bonaguide . . . Tyler's father . . . the bank manager."

"He's your uncle? That means you're engaged to your—?"

She held up her hand. "He's not really my uncle. He just holds my family's purse strings."

"Really? So, Bonaguide controls your life?"

"Sort of," she admitted. "I was supposed to receive my inheritance at eighteen, but Uncle Bonny wanted me to go to college."

"You didn't want to go to college?"

"Yes, but I wasn't really interested in studying higher math."

Jack furrowed his brow. "But you're good at it?"

"That's what Uncle Bonny said, so I went to Harvard."

"But you didn't receive your inheritance, because . . ." he asked, trailing off the last bit.

"I would've when I turned twenty-one, but Uncle Bonny was unhappy that I had changed my major."

"Is it legal for him to withhold your money?"

"According to Tyler it is. Apparently he may hold my

inheritance until I'm thirty." She dropped the shell into the waves.

"So, you're really poor little Margie?"

She shrugged at his deduction. "It's all in how you look at it, Jack. I don't feel poor. I'm having a good time. And I have a large allowance." Then she announced, "I'm hungry."

"And what would you like me to do about that, catch you a fish with my hands?"

"The Wal-Mart bag is beneath the pilot seat in the airplane. It has my granola bars in it."

"I suppose you want me to swim out there and fetch them for you."

"You would do that for me?" She tilted her head in gratitude. "Thank you."

His face wrinkled with a scowl as he got to his feet. Then he removed his T-shirt and unbuckled his belt.

Margie shot him a wary look. "You don't have to skinny dip, Jack. I can go get them myself."

He laughed as he handed her his belt and shirt. "You're still a little prude, Margie." He walked toward the water's edge and waded in his jeans until he came close to the plane.

When he was waist-deep in the sea, Margie called, "Watch out for those dark blue areas."

Jack looked back at her. "Why?"

"Luska."

"What's a Luska?"

Apparently, he didn't know the island myth, so she called out to explain. "It's not a *what*, exactly, it's the name of a sea monster that drags you into its nest and eats you."

Jack nodded. "Thanks for the warning." He walked as far as he could and then swam the rest of the way. Margie watched him pull himself up on the wing and then yank on the door latch of the plane. Once the door opened, Jack fell backward into the water again.

The sun winked off the windshield and Margie waded into the surf to watch Jack surface and pull himself into the plane. Quickly, he came out again with the Wal-Mart bag in his hand.

She hollered, "Don't let the snack bars get wet!"

Even with the distance between them, she saw him glower at her words, but he held the bag upward as he did a sort of dog paddle toward shore. When he was waist-deep in the tide, he began to trudge forward. Suddenly, he fell.

Margie gasped, thinking her granola might be ruined, but Jack kept the bag above the surface of the waves. He looked behind him and then stumbled once more.

"What is wrong with you?" Margie asked, wading further out.

"I've caught my pant leg on something," he told her, yanking forward. He took maybe five steps and then stumbled again. "Take the bag!" he hollered and tossed it to her.

Margie threw it toward shore. "Can I help you?"

"No, I've got it," he told her, bending and tugging.

Suddenly, he disappeared in the shallow water.

Margie's chest constricted. "Jack?" He didn't resurface. "Jack!" She stood waist-deep too and now stepped toward the spot where he'd disappeared.

All at once Jack jumped from the sea. "*Luska!*" he hollered and fell back into the water.

Margie had never really believed in the island myth of Luska, but the way Jack staggered and shouted, she started to reconsider. Spinning in the water, she raced toward the sand, until a slithering and powerful tentacle slipped around her ankle and dragged her down into the water. . . .

Margie surfaced with Luska's skull in a headlock. Ripping and tearing, she all but yanked the beast bald before she realized it was Jack joking around in the waves. When she released him, he fell backward into the surf.

She approached his floating body and touched his shoulder. "How are you doing?" she asked in a weak voice.

"Go away, Margie."

He was alive, that was the important thing. Now she needed to put some distance between them.

"You better keep running," Jack warned, getting to his feet.

Back on her rock, Margie watched Jack stare at the ocean again. According to the position of the sun, the tide change, and the earth's tilt on its axis, they had been marooned for four hours and two minutes. At least that was what her bangle watch read.

Slipping off the boulder, she stared at the palm leaves above her. She didn't notice her financial papers were finally dry. Nor did she notice that, when she took a step backward, her foot kicked the rock she had placed on top of them, and now her report blew across the sand. One paper caught her eye as it fluttered near the boulder. Margie raced to snatch it up but the page kept sailing past her reach. It blew toward Jack and stuck to the back of his damp muscle shirt. He apparently didn't notice anything amiss and Margie thought to tiptoe toward him and simply peel it off his back without him noticing.

Jack turned when he caught her movement just to his left. Frowning suspiciously, he twisted around to see her fully.

The paper sailed off with the breeze again and Margie lunged for it. Jack panicked as he frantically tried to move out of Margie's way. Because he flapped in every direction, Margie tripped over his muscular legs and landed on top of him. She pushed off to make one last grab at the paper before it flew off into the ocean. Crawling, Margie snatched it and held it up in triumph.

"I can't feel anything!" Jack shouted. "I can't feel anything!"

Dropping her arms, Margie looked at him in wonder. "What is wrong with you?" she asked, straightening, and shaking the sand off her paper. "You're not hurt."

Grunting, he rolled to all fours, wobbled like a wet dog, and then declared, "You charged me like a Roman gladiator."

She shook the document at him. "These happen to be very important papers, Jack. If I go home without them I'll positively hear about it."

"Oh, really?" he moaned in an apathetic tone. "What's so important about your little stack there?" He got to his feet.

Before she knew it, he had snatched the entire report from her hands. Margie made a grab for it but missed. Jack turned his back to keep her away. "Now what do we have here?" She made several attempts to recover the document but Jack kept her at arm's length. "Is this yours?"

"It's none of your business."

"None of my business?" His dark eyes narrowed in the bright sunlight.

"After all you've put me through I think I deserve to know you a little better." He turned to the last page and the bottom line. "Wow, you're really rolling in it, aren't you? Or you will be when you're thirty."

Margie wilted with her hands at her sides.

Jack faced her, and tilting his head, he asked, "Why are you carrying this around in the first place? Do you want every thief to know how much you're worth?"

"It was in my purse, tucked away, so every thief *wouldn't* know how much I'm worth. What did you think I was doing at the bank?"

"Waiting for your next victim."

Margie mumbled, "A pox on your ranch and all your belongings," and then plopped in the sand to stare at the ocean.

Jack hunkered down to eye her suspiciously. "What did you say? What did you say . . . something about a pox?"

"Will you relax?"

He took a breath. "I just want to know what to expect next, is all." Finally, he sat in the sand beside her and looked at the papers again. "So, you're just keeping accounts then?"

"If you must know, I ordered the report for my lawyer, okay?"

"Your lawyer-boyfriend, you mean?"

She hesitated for a moment and then confessed, "It's for the prenuptial agreement."

Jack caught her eyes, held them for a moment, and then laughed out loud. "Prenuptials?"

"Yes, prenuptials."

He sobered slightly. "Hey, I don't blame you." After leafing through the papers once more, he handed them to her. "You need to know if a man loves you or your money, right?"

"Wrong. I know Tyler loves me."

"Because he gave you such a beautiful ring?"

Margie stared at her pinkie ring and twisted it around and around.

When she didn't reply, Jack asked, "Don't you want to get married?"

Jack Ivan wasn't exactly the person she wanted to confide in. Still, they might be stuck on this island for the rest of their lives and he would probably hound her to death until she confessed everything, so she admitted, "I've never had much of a chance to think about whether I wanted to get married or not."

"What do you mean?"

She rested her chin on the palm of her hand and her elbow on her bent knee. "It seems I've known Tyler forever. Maybe everyone assumed we would marry, but I was surprised when he popped the question at the dinner table, and in front of my family and twenty other guests. The entire houseful started to cheer, some even cried, and I said . . . yes."

Jack didn't laugh at her as she had expected. She'd thought he would tease her. Instead he asked, "Why didn't you tell him you needed to think about it?"

"I couldn't," she answered, twisting around. "Not in front of all the guests. My father would have been embarrassed and Tyler's mother would have fainted."

"You couldn't speak to him after dinner?"

Margie folded her papers, first this way, then that. "He left with everyone else and there hasn't been much of a chance since then. He's very busy now because of the campaign, and he would like a quick wedding so he can concentrate on his run for election."

"Do you think he's marrying you because it will look good on his ticket?"

Margie cringed in horror. "No!" She *had* thought of it, of course, but she didn't want Jack suggesting it.

Jack raised his brows at her scorching answer.

"He would like the wedding taken care of before the election, that's all."

"Okay," Jack told her with a shrug.

"You're so cynical, Jack. You think all I have to offer a man is money and a good name?"

He shook his head and stared at her. "I didn't say—"

"Well, you're wrong. I've got plenty to offer. As a matter of fact, Tyler has told me many times he loves my mind."

"Your *mind*?"

Margie whirled in the sand to stand up. "What do you mean by that?"

"I was just thinking I appreciated your body first," he said defensively, leaning back to have a look at her hovering over him. "I'm a red-blooded male."

"You would marry a woman because she has a nice body?"

"I would take it into consideration, yes. And don't take your frustrations out on me, Margie."

"I'm not frustrated."

He barked a quick laugh and then stared at the ocean. "You ran off with me quick enough."

"You threatened me."

"But I didn't threaten you today, did I?" He still didn't look at her but she could see his brown eyes sparkle from the glittering water. "You volunteered to fly me to Nassau."

"I'm just keeping close track of you so I'm sure to get my one hundred and fifty-three dollars back."

Now he looked at her with his dark eyes narrowed. His thick lashes nearly touched. Margie could see a slight freckling of his skin. His long and dark hair was drying and it lifted in the breeze. "Are you sure?" he asked in a quiet voice. "Are you sure that's the only reason you helped me?" His broad mouth held no hint of their joking banter. His arm slipped around her waist suddenly and Jack pulled her stomach hard against his shoulder and chest. He looked up at her from his position in the sand. His chin was even with her throat.

Margie placed her palms on his muscled shoulders to balance herself. When she did, Jack's free hand found her hair and twisted her around until she fell into his lap. Then his lips covered hers in a powerful kiss.

"Hello!" called a voice in a megaphone. The boat's motor sounded from around the bend of the island. The voice came again, "Hello?"

Chapter Five

The tiny police station was in an uproar. Nearly fifty men had been arrested the night before at an island festival. They stood in three cells all jammed together like packaged sardines. With no air conditioning, the smell of their boozy breath permeated the room with the help of huge ceiling fans. Two officers stood on duty. One man handed Jack and Margie a ten-page report to fill out, and the other directed them toward a table beneath the only window in the single-story building. The Bahamian government and the president of the United States wanted to know why a perfectly good Cessna had to land in twelve feet of water off Andros Island. Jack explained, "It was all Amelia Earhart's idea."

Margie sat, took a pen from her purse, and observed the men behind the bars. They spoke melodic English with a strange dialect—except for one man who was obviously American. He had a bushy mustache and was dressed for a costume party. A large feathered hat sat upon his head.

86

She stared at him for a moment.

The man returned her stare, looking as if he was very tired of this whole ordeal. Two men on either side of him examined his cell phone.

Jack captured her attention when he turned a chair backward to straddle it. "Is this going to take long?"

She knew why he asked. He was eager to hunt for Brittany again. "It will take as long as it takes. Stop harassing me." She tapped the end of her pen on the Formica tabletop.

"I wasn't harassing—"

Margie blurted out the only thing on her mind. "Why did you kiss me?"

"What's that?" He had been eyeing the men in the nearby cell.

"Why did you kiss me?"

He gave her a careful smile while his brown eyes concentrated on her lips. "I don't know. I guess I just wanted to show you what some things are about."

"Things? What things?" She leaned against the table now. "You think I've never been kissed?"

Jack leaned in as well. "A kiss on the cheek doesn't count." He grinned, pleased with his answer.

"Other men . . . I've been kissed by other men. Tyler . . ."

"Tyler has kissed you like that, has he? When? When he dropped that bombshell of a proposal on you last month?" He looked so smug. "Has the governor wannabe really kissed you like I kissed you, Margie?"

No, he hadn't, but it was none of Jack's business.

He chuckled at her hesitation. "You liked it."

Add arrogance to the list of things she disliked about Jack. The conversation would go nowhere, so Margie replied, "Never mind." She studied the report in front of her and filled in her name and address. Tapping her pen again, she charged, "I just don't get it, Jack. How can you kiss me like that when you don't even like me?"

Jack rubbed his eyes and then leaned his chin into the palm of his hand. "Who said I don't like you? After all, we spent last night together. It's natural I think of you in that way." He mocked her by wiggling his eyebrows up and down.

A benevolent character came to Margie's defense. "You're maligning the girl, Jack. Explain yourself."

Margie spun around to see who stood up for her. Within earshot stood a tall black man grinning at her with his very white and crooked teeth. He had poked his forearms through the cell bars. The left side of his face looked newly injured, and dried blood caked in the corner of his swollen lip.

Jack frowned. Disregarding the man, he hissed, "I just told you why I kissed you."

"No, you didn't."

The argument drew interest from other men and they approached the bars grinning in the same manner as the first man. Even the American seemed captivated at the unfolding scene. He grabbed his cell phone from the other men's hands.

Jack stood and pointed a finger at all of them. "This

is none of your business." He glared at Margie and then placed both hands on the table to lean toward her. "Will you hurry up so we can get out of here?" Abruptly, as though he didn't trust her to respond quickly, Jack snatched her purse to look for another pen. While searching, he declared, "I kissed you because I wanted to kiss you."

His voice raised a fraction. "Once I started kissing you, I didn't want to stop because it felt good, okay? I admit it. *You're hot!*"

He shouted the last bit and Margie winced. He didn't have to tell everyone for cripes sake. She tried to keep her voice even. "Don't you wonder what Brittany will think when she finds out you kissed me?"

Jack stopped his search to stare at Margie. "Brittany? Who cares what Brittany thinks about it?" And then his hand found something interesting. "What the . . ."

Margie looked up and recognized her two-carat engagement ring pinched between Jack's index finger and thumb. "Give that to me!" She lunged across the table to grab it.

He held his arm high. "Well, you weren't lying after all. You are engaged." Margie made a second grab and nearly knocked over the table.

Jack studied the triangular-cut, 100-point, faceted diamond while keeping Margie at arm's length. "This brings up an interesting question, don't you think?" His dark eyes narrowed as he watched Margie sprawled halfway across the table. "Why did you kiss me?" He raised one brow with the question.

Margie shoved backward and straightened her pink blouse. "You kissed me," she reminded him irritably.

"Oh, come on, darling. You kissed me too. I don't remember any struggling on your part. As a matter of fact," he looked at the men behind bars, "I tried to pull away but she wrapped her arms tighter around me." He told the story like the innocent victim, and while he was lost in his lie, Margie snatched the ring out of his hand and shoved it into her purse again.

The man who first defended her said, "Explain yourself, Margie. Professing love to two men is no way to go through life."

How quickly men stuck together!

Margie faced her accuser. "Oh, really? Well, drunk and beat up is no way to go through life either, pal, so butt out."

That did it. While Jack laughed boisterously and fell against the table, twenty men began to whoop and holler and create a general uproar.

The upheaval caught the attention of Officer Peety at the front desk. He walked toward the back of the room to investigate. "What's going on here?"

Margie whistled beneath her breath, grabbed her pen and papers, and returned to the work at hand.

Eyeing Jack, Peety's hand went to the club on his belt. "Heckling the prisoners is not permitted."

Jack's expression fell. "Heckling? I didn't heckle anyone."

Officer Peety looked at Margie to confirm Jack's claim.

When she opened her mouth to answer, Jack spoke over her. "Don't ask her anything."

The policeman pulled the nightstick from his belt. "Take a seat, sir."

Pausing, Margie chided, "Will you stop making trouble? The sooner you quit fooling around the quicker I can finish this report and we can get out of here."

Stunned into silence, Jack dropped into his seat and closed his eyes. Margie nodded at the officer in a respectful gesture to let him know she could handle the situation from there. Peety returned the nod and walked toward the bars to quiet the prisoners.

Continuing with her report, she stopped to ask: "Is 'Jack Ivan was no help at all' a complete sentence?" When Jack didn't answer, Margie glanced across the table at him. She did a double take when she saw the stunned look on his face, spun around, and looked where he looked.

Two prisoners had Peety against the bars while another grabbed the keys from the police officer's belt. Once the lock opened, the men began to stream into the room. The fellow with the keys made for the other cell doors to release his friends. The second officer reached for his gun, but too slowly, and one of the rioters grabbed it from him and stuck it in his own belt.

"I'll take that purse," said a very large Bahamian man who looked like he could break furniture with his bare hands.

"Sure," Margie told him, standing now. "Just let me get a few things out of it first."

"Hand it over lady." He smelled like he looked: sweaty and crusty. *Too few people take self-improvement seriously,* Margie thought, and then she recommended, "What you need to do is go out there and get a job instead of resorting to robbery. It would be such a simple change for you."

"Give him the purse," Jack suggested, eyeballing the fellow.

Margie shook her head. "I'm not giving him my ring."

"You don't wear it," Jack reminded her.

Their argument was enough diversion for Jack to overturn the table beside them. He pulled Margie by the arm to yank her out of the way when the would-be robber grabbed his shin and danced on one foot. Another fellow rushed forward and lit the papers on fire.

They huddled at the back of the room as Jack blocked a chair hurtling straight for them. The large Bahamian stopped dancing and took several steps in their direction.

"Let's go, let's go, let's go!" Jack hollered over his shoulder.

"Where?" Margie asked, trying to see the exit.

"Up," Jack told her, indicating the window above her head. Then his arm went around Margie's waist and he elevated her toward the ledge. She grabbed the sill and strained as Jack lifted her hips and derriere.

"Watch your hands!" she shouted at him and then realized there was no way to get down. She looked here and there in the narrow alleyway and saw a Dumpster just to her left. She would've made a jump for it but Jack pushed at her sneakers and she fell out the window.

A moment later, he came down beside her. "Run!" he hollered before she managed to stand.

It wasn't necessary to run because the gigantic fellow coming out the window behind them got stuck halfway. Margie slapped him briskly. "Crazy circus freak!" She slapped him again.

The man raised his big arms to protect himself. When he did, he loosed himself and fell backward inside the building again.

Jack and Margie looked at each other.

"Come on," Jack hissed between clenched teeth. He took her hand and ran toward the end of the alley and out into the street. Prisoners filed out of the station and rioted by turning over trash bins and mailboxes. Civilians on the road stopped to stare. Glass shattered. Somewhere a woman screamed and a police whistle pierced the air.

"We should try to find the airport!" Margie cried over the noise.

"No, we've got to find Brittany's ship."

Even now!

Margie slid to a stop. "Brittany? Our lives are in danger, Jack, and all you can think about is finding Brittany?"

Jack pushed her in front of him. "She is the reason we're here."

Trying to pull an arm loose, Margie reminded him, "She's the reason *you* are here. I'm here because . . ."

Why was she here?

"Someone is following us," Jack told her in a low tone. "Keep walking." He held tight to her elbow and propelled her toward a cigar shop. Margie tried to look behind her but Jack pushed her ahead again. She only caught a glimpse of the Bahamian fellow she had called a circus freak, and how amusing, he had brought along a friend.

The proprietor stood at the window instead of behind the counter. The sweet aroma of tobacco filled the air. Jack asked, "Can you tell us the way to the cruise ship docks?"

"What's going on out there?" the man asked without taking his eyes off the scene out the window. He was a pale man of about fifty.

"Someone started a riot," Jack told him, eyeing Margie accusingly. "Come on," he rushed the man. "Which way to the docks?"

"West," the proprietor told him, ignoring them now that the rioters were moving his way. He opened the cash register and began stuffing money in every pocket of his shirt and trousers.

Jack led Margie into the street again, spotted a taxi, and raced toward it. He slapped the hood of the car, and hollered through the opened passenger-side window. "We need to get to the docks!"

"Do you know how to get there?" the driver asked in a clearly American accent.

Margie bent to see him but the driver shifted sideways. Jack opened the door and motioned for her to get inside. "All I know is to go west, pal," he told the driver and jumped into the seat beside Margie.

On the back of the driver's seat was the operator's license showing a slender black man with a spray of dark freckles across his cheeks. Margie tried again to see the driver but her attention quickly shifted to the large Bahamian trying to open her door.

The cab driver punched the accelerator, sending the car forward and scattering pedestrians out of the street and onto the walkway. They scattered again when the cabbie drove on the sidewalk.

Out the back window, Margie witnessed the Bahamian men hailing their own cab. She would have mentioned they were being followed again, but when Margie twisted around in the seat, she saw Jack's expression. His eyes stared ahead unblinkingly. Maybe crash landings and jailhouse riots were too much for a cattleman to handle in one day.

Five minutes later the cab skidded to a stop in a blacktop parking lot. Huge ships were berthed in the harbor. Each had its name written on the side in large swirling letters.

Before the car came to a complete stop, Jack burst out of the car and raced for the *Dolphin*'s gangplank.

Margie almost forgot about paying the driver. When she turned around with her purse in hand, the cab had already moved away toward the far end of the parking lot.

A Norwegian officer stood guard at the ship's plank. "There's no one on board but the crew, sir," the officer told Jack. "All the passengers are at a luau on Little

Abaco." He stood tall, about the same height as Jack. His thin arms stuck out of his uniform like twigs on a young tree.

"Little Abaco? How do we get to it?"

"By boat," Margie answered, pulling Jack away from the landing. "There's a ferry service not far from here."

By the time Jack and Margie reached the ferry and took the boat ride to Little Abaco, the sun had begun to set in the pink sky. The clear water melted into a deep turquoise in the fading daylight.

Jack stood at the railing. Margie approached him while smoothing out the material of her bright top and flowered pants. She still wore her hair in a ponytail but could feel the tendrils sticking to her cheeks. It hadn't been a glamorous day.

"We're almost there," she told him, meaning to cheer him up. "And we've made it without injury or casualty. Good for us."

Jack cupped his chin and balanced his elbow on the railing. With his thumb, he rubbed his full bottom lip. In the low light, his features took on a stern and rough appearance. His dark eyes were shadowed. "I've been standing here remembering how our little adventure together began." Straightening, he placed both hands on the wood railing.

Margie leaned next to Jack and faced him. "A collision in the bank lobby."

"That's right. It's all been one big collision."

A tall Bahamian man offered them a glass of punch but Jack and Margie declined. Neither of them saw how he nodded to one of his associates across the deck.

Jack smiled but didn't seem to mean it. "Let me see if I can paint a word-picture for you, Margie, about what it's like to know you." He turned his face toward the darkening sky to think for a moment. Then he said, "You're like a ten-car pileup on the interstate while I'm trying to get somewhere. I'm not dead, but I'm in shock, and I'm suffering."

Margie offered a quick grin. "That's a funny way to put it."

"Funny?" His dark eyebrows shot skyward. "Funny is not a word I would use to describe any part of our adventure together." He took a step toward her.

Margie took a step backward. She offered, "Oh, I don't know, I thought it was sort of funny when—"

"Nothing was funny."

She didn't like the fierce look in Jack's eyes. He would probably need to see a doctor, maybe get a prescription.

"Sit down," he instructed, directing her down into a deck chair. Then he bent to carefully explain, "You need to understand, Margie. My life is very different from yours. My life is boring, okay? I like boring. I like knowing what's going to happen next." She opened her mouth to reason with him but Jack shook his head. "Don't talk to me just now."

She wanted to reassure him. She had Tylenol in her

purse if he needed it. But when she started to tell him, Jack shushed her by placing his index finger on her mouth.

Gently, he patted her lips. "Just stay right here."

Once the ferry docked, Margie followed Jack into the street, where he hailed a taxi. They rode in silence toward the beach.

The taxi took a circular drive and parked next to a thatched hut. Standing outside the cab, Margie heard the mellow ring of steel drums. The sea crashed to shore in the distance and sprayed the breeze with salt. They walked a stone path lined with palm, bottlebrush, and hibiscus flowers. Tiki torches lit the way.

Margie slowed when she saw the shore and the mass of people attending the luau. Five huts lined the sand and the torches illuminated the area in a soft yellow glow. There were at least a thousand guests mingling on the beach. It would be no easy task to find the girl.

But that didn't stop Jack from trying. "We'll start at the first hut."

While he scanned the area, Margie lingered at a table near the bonfire. A pig's head lay displayed on a platter. Hibiscus flowers and a garland of fruit surrounded the plate. The rest of the pig roasted on a spit further down the beach. When Jack turned to face Margie again, she suggested, "We can split up and narrow the search if you like." She accepted a tall glass of punch from a passing waiter.

Margie would've lifted the drink to her mouth but

Jack pulled the plastic cup from her lips. "We didn't pay to get in here."

"I haven't had anything to eat since the granola bar on the island," she complained. Her stomach growled with the smell of roast pork. Bowls of salad sat spread out on another table.

"Quit worrying about your stomach," he told her, grabbing her hand. "And stay with me. There's no telling what will happen if you're left alone." They walked along the shoreline and avoided a large woman dressed in a muumuu. She had big bushy hair and very red lips . . . and a mustache?

"Do you remember what Brittany looks like?" Jack asked without noticing the woman. "She's tall and—"

"Pretty. I remember."

Jack turned in the sand to shoot her a quizzical look. "Pretty? Yes, she's pretty."

"That's what you said."

"I know." He hadn't quit frowning at her, but suddenly the music caught his attention and he quickened his pace toward a makeshift dance floor. The steel drum band sat on a platform within the tent. One man sang while three others played their instruments.

"Do you see her?" Margie asked over the music.

"There's a tall brunette in the middle of the floor. It could be her." Jack shifted his weight and tried to see over many heads. "Come on," he told her, pulling her into his arms to dance toward the center of the crowd.

It surprised Margie that he pulled her close. It made her think of the kiss they shared and her belly quivered with an odd excitement. Jack's strong hand stayed in the center of her back and she gazed up at his handsome features.

They danced a two-step swing and as the crowd thickened, Jack pulled her closer still and held her hand against his chest. Margie placed her free hand on his shoulder. "Do you see her yet?"

Her question distracted Jack and he gazed into Margie's eyes. He seemed to try to look away again but his dark eyes returned to her face. His hand in the middle of her back moved down slightly and then his arms tightened as his thumb caressed Margie's fingers.

The moonlight worked its magic, and the steel drums struck a familiar chord in her heart. Margie fell hard for Jack right then, right there beneath the star-filled Bahamian sky. In his arms was where she fit and where she knew she belonged forever.

Jack's features softened and his eyes considered Margie's lips like he wanted to kiss her again. "You're not looking for Brittany," he accused.

"Oh," she answered softly, forgetting all about their search. "I can't see over the crowd."

Jack's throat muscle constricted when he swallowed and Margie moved her hand to feel the strong pulse beating there.

Their eyes locked as they swayed with the tune.

"You should pay more attention," he admonished in a husky voice. "Brittany could be right here and we'll miss her."

"Who's Brittany?"

"I don't remember right now," he murmured and brought his face closer to hers. His thick eyelashes lowered and his features began to blur. He was near enough for Margie to feel his warm breath on her lips. They stopped dancing and the couples nearby seemed to fade far away into the surrounding night. Even the drums quieted. Margie could only hear the beat of her own heart. She didn't notice when the music stopped playing or that the other couples stopped dancing to listen to an announcement.

"The Hupa Ceremony begins in five minutes. Participants, please make your way to the Civic Hall."

Jack leaned his forehead against hers and she longed for him to kiss her, but instead he said, "We're getting distracted."

The music began again as several couples left the floor. Jack took Margie's hand and led her onto the sand. The air smelled tangy and warm and a soft breeze touched her hair. Margie tripped lightly and it caused her to take her eyes off Jack for a moment. "There she is!"

Jack spun around. "Brittany?"

Margie pointed toward the Civic Hall and the gathering crowd lining up to go inside.

The room was small, especially with one hundred and fifty people jammed side-by-side. Each woman who entered the hall received a wreath after she signed her name at the registration table. Margie signed for both her and Jack and hoped to get a larger prize later; a larger prize like a week-long holiday at the Port Lucaya Resort and

Yacht Club, dinner for two at some local restaurant, or a General Electric toaster.

A small black woman handed Margie a garland and she took it happily. It would be her only souvenir of this unplanned vacation. Slipping the flowers over her head, she asked Jack, "You don't think they offered one of these to the pig before his little ceremony, do you?"

He laughed and pulled on her hand to walk through the crowd, squeezing his way past people. He headed for the opposite side of the room. "I think I see Brittany against the wall. Stay close."

Margie winced when a microphone caused the dated sound-system to squeal. All eyes turned toward the man who stood on the platform in the front of the room. At first, Margie thought he spoke with the same dialect as the men at the police station, but then he began to speak in a foreign language. She only understood a word here and there.

Jack towed her through a sea of couples who paid them little attention and who concentrated raptly on the speaker. Standing in pairs, they wore smiles, and some shed tears. To her left a pair of black men stood watching her.

Margie recognized them from the jailhouse. They took their eyes off her and pretended to watch the speaker. She pulled her purse closer to her side.

Jack reached the far wall without finding Brittany. While he gazed over everyone's heads to find a new direction, Margie continued to watch the ceremony.

The speaker's voice grew louder. She made out the words slowly: "I . . . pronounce . . . man and wife."

Margie jerked her hand from Jack's grip.

The speaker motioned with his arms for the couples to squeeze together.

Men and their brides embraced and kissed.

Jack frowned at Margie. "What's wrong?"

"Oh boy," she breathed out at last.

"What's the matter?"

"Well," she answered, licking her dry lips. "I think we just got married."

Chapter Six

It took a long time to get out the door, and the woman Margie thought looked like Brittany wasn't Brittany but another dark-haired beauty just as newly wed as Jack and Margie.

Jack dragged Margie through the masses to bawl her out in the moonlight. She presumed the preacher had said for better or worse, and things were getting worse real fast.

"If you knew what the man said, why didn't you tell me to head for the door?" His dark eyes smoldered in the tiki lights.

The pig finished turning on the spit and the steel drums beat out a version of "We've Only Just Begun."

Margie defended herself. "This could hardly be a legal ceremony. We didn't even receive a certificate."

"Excuse me," a woman said coming to stand in front of them. Margie recognized her as the receptionist who had taken their names at the table in the Civic Hall.

"You forgot your certificate. You'll need this to get your name changed, Mrs. Ivan."

Margie stared at the document. This was her big prize? She would rather have had a toaster!

Jack started to laugh then. Not a ha ha, that's so funny sort of laugh, but a maniacal sort of chuckle that caused people to stare at him.

"Come on, Jack," Margie suggested, "you had better sit down."

He did, right in the sand.

Margie walked toward a bench near the cement wall. She turned to see Jack sitting on the ground. Couples walked around him and stared at him like he was drunk. Tramping back, she told him, "I'll get you a drink."

When she returned, she pushed a tall glass of punch at him. "Here."

"What is it?"

"I don't know. It smells like . . ." She took a sniff. "Insect repellant."

His snigger sounded stiff and feigned. "First you marry me, now you're trying to kill me."

"Pull yourself together, Jack." Margie sat in the sand next to him, careful with the glass. If it spilled, there would be no insect life left on the island. "Think about it. What sense does it make for me to kill you? I have no motive."

He sobered completely then and his dark eyes traced Margie's moonlit features. "That's right, you have no motive, but I do."

Margie held up the certificate to see the printing in the tiki lights. "This isn't real. We're not married."

Scrambling in the sand to get to his feet, Jack snatched the paper from her hand and held the document close to his face. "It's notarized. It's a marriage certificate with our names on it, and it's seal-punched." He let the paper fall into her lap. "We are married."

Getting to her feet, Margie followed Jack toward the water's edge. "Where are you going?"

"I have to think."

She pursued him along the shoreline for several feet and then said, "Maybe we're only married in the Bahamas. In the States, I'm still Margie. . . ." Jack stopped to glare at her. "That is the dumbest thing I've ever heard." His eyes flashed in the moonlight like the thousands of tiny stars pin-dotted above their heads.

Margie lifted her voice above the pounding surf. "Really? Do you want to know the dumbest thing I've ever heard?" She didn't wait for his reply. " 'You have to help me, Margie. I have to stop Brittany. It's the most important thing I'll ever do in my life.' "

Jack spun around to face her squarely. With narrowing eyes, he chanted, " 'Ring of mine, pink and sublime. I'll ruin Jack's life until the end of time.' "

"That's not the way it goes."

Jack gritted his teeth. Shutting his eyes, he spit out, "I don't want to fight about it." Pressing his hands to his face, he rubbed hard. "Here's what we'll do: We'll get the marriage annulled and we'll part ways. We'll pretend we never met. If I see you on the street, I'll say to myself, now there's a pretty girl, but I won't be tempted to stop and make conversation because I know what conversation with you leads to."

"You're babbling," Margie cautioned.

"I know I'm babbling." He faced her again with bright eyes. "Who are you, Margie? The angel of death? You've tried six ways to kill me."

"You begged me to help you."

" 'I begged you to help me,' " he repeated in a serene voice. "Engrave that on my headstone, will you?"

A line of taxis waited in the circular driveway to transport luau guests back to the ferryboats. The party broke up and several couples walked toward the vehicles. Jack's hand held the latch of one cab when he spotted Brittany.

Marching toward the woman, he apparently forgot all about Margie. Margie didn't follow him this time. They were supposed to pretend they'd never met, so she climbed into the back of a cab and shut the door. Out the back window, she watched Jack fall to the pavement when the tall blond man accompanying Brittany slugged him on the jaw.

Sitting in the vacant Bahamas Air terminal, Margie considered what to do next. Several hotels lined the street outside the airport and she thought about booking a room for the night since the next flight to Miami took off at nine-thirty in the morning. She lifted her purse and Wal-Mart bag and walked toward the ladies' restroom.

When the door shut behind her, Jack ran past heading for the ticket counter.

"Can you tell me if someone booked a flight to Miami?" he asked the agent.

"Everyone on vacation has booked a flight to Miami," the redhead answered distractedly and then looked up at Jack. She smiled. "What's the name?" She stood nearly as tall as Jack and wore her hair in a tight bun that pulled at the skin around her eyes.

His thoughts were sluggish and now his jaw ached. "Margie," he answered, rubbing his face and scratching the bristle of beard beneath his hand.

"Last name?"

"Ivan?"

The woman glanced at the screen and shook her head. "No, no Margie Ivan on tomorrow's flight list."

"How about another Margie or Margaret without the Ivan?"

"No Margaret," she answered. "I see a Mary. . . ."

Jack's fingers drummed the counter. "No, her name is Margie." Frustrated, he leaned over the counter to see the computer screen for himself. "What's the name of the lawyer in that commercial? You know, the one with the good-looking ambulance chaser sitting in a library talking about what to do if you get injured in an accident. Do you know who I'm talking about? He's running for governor."

"Sir, I have no idea who you're talking about." The agent lost her smile and turned the computer monitor out of his line of vision. "Would you like to buy a ticket?"

Jack smacked the counter with the palm of his hand. "No, I don't want to buy a ticket. I want to find my wife." He moved away, just missing Margie as she walked through the automatic doors and out into the night.

She booked a room at the Radisson, registered under her full name of Mary Margaret Walker, and took room 316.

Jack sat on the double bed in room 317 at the Radisson hotel across the street from the airport. He had dialed every hotel in the area asking for Margie but did not find her. Now he ordered room service. His stomach growled from lack of food. With no clean clothes to change into, he showered and grabbed a terry robe off the bathroom door. He had no plans to go back to the airport that night, so he sat on the bed to wait for his food.

Margie's skin felt dry from the day's exposure to the sun. After a quick shower, she wrapped herself in the terry robe hanging on the back of the bathroom door, pulled her hair into a towel, and applied a thick layer of Noxzema cream to her face. Her green eyes and pink lips were all that remained visible.

A quick rap on the door startled her and she tiptoed toward it. Spying through the peephole, she didn't see anyone and inched the door open. The smell of hamburger and fries wafted toward her nostrils as her stomach pinched in hunger. She took the tray of food inside without noticing the wiry-haired fellow unlocking room 314, still dressed in a muumuu and Hawaiian lei.

Margie flipped on the evening news and watched the coverage of the local riot. She patted the burger with her napkin to remove excess grease. It wasn't a veggie burger and it tasted wonderful.

"I ordered dinner forty-five minutes ago." Jack stood near the door with the phone cord stretched out behind him. "You didn't deliver it, it's not here." He looked into the hallway again to make sure he hadn't missed it.

Two very large Bahamian men in Room 315 opened their door, looked startled to see Jack, and then slammed the door.

Frowning, Jack leaned against the jam. "Did I pay for it? Look pal, I want my burger and fries."

The phone fell off the bedside table and clattered to the carpet. Leaving the door ajar, Jack backstepped and laid the phone on the table again. "Just send another plate of food up, okay?" Dropping the receiver into the cradle, he walked toward the door again to push it shut. He paused when he heard the sound of a television in the next room. Tapping on the door of 316, Jack waited for someone to answer the door.

Margie chewed the last fry. When she heard the knock at the door, she took the empty plate and the platter and handed everything to the man standing there. She never looked at his face, and after she shut the door, she returned to her spot in front of the television.

Jack stared at the door, terrified by the woman who had opened and shut it so quickly. He didn't know what was wrong with her face but it seemed her thick white skin *peeled* from her face in huge strips. Then he looked at the empty plate knowing he had lost his appetite.

Margie laid her head straight on the pillow so as not to smear her Noxzema-coated face. She closed her eyes without thinking about locking the door, and she fell asleep immediately.

She woke when something bumped the bedside table.

It took her only a second to wake and then she realized her cell phone was ringing. Margie reached for it and remained blissfully unaware of the very large Bahamian man crouching at her footboard. He crawled toward her purse on the chest of drawers.

"Margie?" the voice on the phone crackled.

She shook the phone and replaced it to her ear. "Tyler? It's . . ." She leaned to see the red numbers on the clock radio. "Two o'clock in the morning."

"I've been trying to reach you all evening. The service says you're out of range. Why are you out of range?"

"I'm in Nassau."

"For a wedding cake?"

Margie swung her feet to the floor and grabbed her purse from the chest of drawers. She didn't see the shoes sticking out from beneath the heavy curtains. When she turned toward the bed again, she missed the man climbing out onto the windowsill and slipping onto the ledge. "No, no wedding cake this time. I'll tell you about it tomorrow."

"You always say that, Margie. You tell me, 'I'll tell you tomorrow,' and then you spin off some story of misadventure that's frankly unbelievable."

"They're all true stories, Tyler."

He dismissed her statement. Scathingly, he asked, "What was it this time? Did your car break down? Did you have to buy a ticket home on Delta and then get marooned on a deserted island only to get picked up by the Coast Guard and dropped off in the Bahamas?"

Margie screwed up her face in amazement. "That's surprisingly accurate, except the Delta part." She searched the bottom of her purse for her engagement ring and slipped it on her finger.

"You know, Margie. I'm beginning to think my father is right."

Margie frowned into the receiver. "Right about what?"

"That you have an alarming ability to take a bad situation and make it worse."

"Uncle Bonny said that?"

It sounded like Tyler took a slow breath. "I wish you wouldn't call him that."

"Sorry," she said, gazing at her ring in the low light.

Even in the semi-darkness, the two-carat stone sparkled. She took it off again and put it into her purse. "I'll be home tomorrow for sure. I'm taking a ten-fifteen flight to Miami and then I'll be home around four. Why don't we have dinner?"

"That's a good idea. I would like to discuss some things with you."

"Really? Like what?"

"Like the way you tear off to Miami without a moment's notice. How does that look, Margie? My political opponent would have a field day with the information. He could already have a tail on you, you know? I hope you haven't gotten into any trouble in Nassau."

"Trouble? I haven't gotten into trouble." Unless he counted falling in love with another man trouble—unless he counted marrying another man in a mass-marriage ceremony trouble. "Listen, Tyler, I'm going to go back to sleep. I will see you tomorrow."

"All right," he responded, ready to hang up. "Before you ring off, did you get the information from the bank—?"

The connection failed then and Margie gladly switched off the phone. Standing, she put her purse on the dresser and then shut the tall window she didn't know she had left opened. The lock snapped when she closed it soundly.

A long and quavering scream sounded outside, as if someone fell from the third floor of the hotel. Margie pulled the curtain aside and stared into the night. Without seeing anything, she replaced the curtains and checked the door before returning to bed.

Wild pink–flowered pants caught Jack's attention the next morning as he grabbed a cup of coffee from the hotel's restaurant. He quickly laid coins on the table, pushed through the rotating door, and ran out onto the street. The sun just peeked over the horizon but many vendors were out and ready to begin the day's business.

He saw another flash of pink round the corner and Jack set his coffee cup on top of a mailbox and ran in the same direction.

A man with bushy hair picked up Jack's coffee and finished it for him. Situating his camera phone, he snapped off another picture while Jack jockeyed for position around the vendors.

Not knowing or caring about Jack's pedestrian problems, Margie bought breakfast, and while Jack juggled between two Bahamian children imploring him to buy a shell necklace, Margie spread strawberry cream cheese on her whole wheat bagel.

She sank her teeth into the first bite and then pulled her plane ticket from her purse. Only a half-hour remained before she could board the aircraft, so she grabbed her purse and bagel, and excused herself around a tall Bahamian man in an arm cast.

At the end of the street, Jack looked left and then right. How could a girl wearing shocking pink and flowered clothing simply disappear? Behind him, Margie left the bagel shop and walked the short distance to the airport terminal. Jack turned in time to see her round the corner and he rushed back through the merchants. It took him nearly five minutes to reach the corner since he bought a shell necklace to keep a young boy from hanging on his leg.

Entering the airport, he headed straight for the Bahamas Air terminal. Few people sat in the lobby. Not seeing Margie, Jack checked the magazine counter. With hands on his hips, he scanned the crowd.

Margie walked into the ladies' room and stood in front of the wide mirror. She had leaned in to study her sun-pinked cheeks when Jack slid into the room behind her. Seeing him in the reflection made her jump and then spin around. "You can't come in here."

He looked so thrilled to see her that Margie thought he meant to kiss her. Instead, he said, "I need to talk to you."

It delighted her to see Jack. She thought she might never again, but there he stood in the women's bathroom with her.

He certainly looked out of place posing in front of the pink and silver wallpaper and baby-changing table. His dark hair glistened in the overhead lighting and his big muscled arms flexed beneath his opened sleeveless plaid shirt. "Do you have the marriage license?"

"You're not still going on about that are you?" She took Jack by the arm to escort him toward the exit. "We're not married, Jack. I'm engaged."

Jack twisted his arm out of Margie's grip and took her by the shoulders. "Do you have it or not?"

Puzzled, Margie looked at her purse.

He released her to snap open the bag.

"Stop!" She rounded on him. "You can't just go through my things like that."

Jack shoved the purse toward her and Margie scowled at him while her hand searched for the document. "I have

CJ Love

a plane to catch, you know? My life doesn't revolve around helping Jack Ivan. I still have to buy a battery for my car and drive back to Tampa . . . Oh! Hold this," she instructed, handing him the flowery garland, the wrapped and half-eaten bagel, and the plane ticket. "I don't see it."

Jack took the purse from her hands and dumped the contents on the counter. "Where is the certificate, Margie?"

"I thought you had it."

"I let it fall into your lap last night on the beach, right after you tried to poison me with bug spray."

Margie crinkled her forehead, trying to remember.

Jack stuffed the items back into her purse in a shoddy manner. She stopped him to do the job herself.

"Think," he encouraged. "What did you do with it?"

Margie still reflected.

Jack asked, "Are you going to eat that?"

She handed him the bagel. "All I remember is you rambling on about committing suicide."

"Yeah," he agreed while he unwrapped the bagel. "I'm still considering that. Did you take the certificate out of your purse last night?"

Margie shifted her weight. "Sure, Jack. I fantasized all night about what it would really be like to be Mrs. Jack Ivan. What do you think?"

"I believe it," he told her, tilting his dark head. "But since it's not here, that means the certificate is still on the beach. Let's go."

"I have a plane to catch."

Jack took her elbow. "Oh, no you don't, Mrs. Ivan.

You're sticking with me. I'm in this mess because of you." He directed her through the automatic doors of the airport.

Marching into the sunshine, Margie tried to keep step with Jack. "Why can't we forget about it? We'll just pretend none of this ever happened. That's what you suggested last night."

He wasn't listening and finally spun around to face her. "You don't understand, Margie. I want to be married to you."

Back on the ferryboat, Jack led Margie to a deck chair. He pulled a seat in front of her. Resting his elbows on his knees, he leaned toward her. In the early morning sunshine, his hair looked freshly washed and wavy. "It's time for me to explain a few things."

It was far past time to explain, but Margie didn't mention it.

"When my father passed away, he left the Flying D to my sister and me. The Flying D is the name of my ranch. Did I ever tell you that?"

Margie watched his fingers press together as he spoke. She shook her head at his question.

"There's never been any problem with the arrangement since Brittany and I both love the ranch."

"Wait a minute," Margie stopped him. "Your sister's name is Brittany too?"

"My sister is the only Brittany I know."

Margie pulled a face. "You mean we've been chasing your sister all this time? I thought . . ."

"What?"

"I thought you chased after Brittany because you were in love with her and she left you for another man."

Now it was his turn to frown. Standing, he raked a hand through his long hair. "I would never chase after a woman who blew me off like that."

Margie stood too. "Well, you certainly let me think that was the case." Then, she mimicked, " 'I have to stop Brittany, it may already be too late, she's probably already married.' Why do you think I asked you if Brittany cared if you kissed me?"

Jack shook his head. "You say a lot of stuff that doesn't make sense." He fell back into the deck chair. Pointing at the other, he offered, "Please sit down and let me finish."

Margie sat in wonderment; Jack wasn't in love with Brittany?

"Brittany has always taken care of the finances. I take care of the daily operation of the ranch by supervising the men, that sort of thing. It had been a fine setup until Brittany came to me last week and told me she had fallen in love with Andrew McDonald."

"Your neighbor?"

"Very good," Jack nodded. "You remember." Placing his hands on his thighs, he continued. "I don't trust McDonald. He's made several offers on the property because of the water resources on my land."

"You think he would marry your sister to get the land?" When Jack nodded, Margie asked, "What possible advantage would that give him? You would still be half-owner of the property, right?"

Jack stood again and leaned his back on the ship's railing. "My father stipulated very clearly in his will that whoever married first had the decision power regarding the ranch. Marriage matured a person, he thought." He leaned toward Margie. "Do you see? By marrying Brittany, Andrew will have the decision power to absorb my land into his, or at least he'll try to talk Brittany into joining the properties together. She has always had an eye for money. The Flying D struggles financially from time to time. McDonald will pour his substantial money into it and I will lose all control over the ranch."

"But it would be lucrative?"

"Financially secure or not, the Flying D is my family's home."

Unexpectedly, he grinned. "But, I don't have to worry about it anymore, Margie. You and I married first." His dark brown eyes glinted. "Andrew and Brittany won't marry until later today. And once I prove we married last night, Andrew will reveal his true intentions and call off the wedding."

He straightened and stared at Little Abaco, now just off the portside. "That's why we have to find the marriage certificate."

The ferry docked and they made their way back to the beach. The luau tents and band platform had been removed from the area. No tiki torches lined the stone path. White waves pounded the shore as Jack and Margie kicked sand toward the Civic Hall.

Jack stopped. "We were right about here, don't you think?" Margie studied the prints in the sand. "It's hard to say." She looked toward the municipal building. "Maybe we could just get a copy of the certificate. Do you think they're open?"

"Let's look around first. It could've blown over by the trees." Jack headed for the thick brushy area.

While he stomped through the hibiscus, Margie found a bench to sit on to wait for him. She set her belongings on the seat next to her. "Try looking over in that direction," she instructed, swinging her feet. "You should probably watch for snakes." She drew a circle in the white sand with the toe of her sneaker.

Jack lifted his head out of the bushes. "What are you doing?"

Margie paused from her sand art. "Waiting."

"For what? Come help me. We don't have a lot of time."

"But there are bugs out there, probably spiders too, what do you want to bet?"

Jack glowered at her, which meant he was getting cranky again, so Margie got to her feet. The Wal-Mart bag nearly fell when she stood and she made a grab for it. That was when she saw the blue certificate crammed next to her granola bars.

Oh, Jack would be mad about this.

Margie held the document behind her back as she shuffled her way through the sand toward the shrubbery. She pretended to look for a moment and then said, "I found it," and held out the paper for Jack to see.

He grabbed the document out of her hand. "Yes!" he exclaimed, trudging his way out of the bushes. "Where did you find it?"

Pointing imprecisely at the general area, she answered, "Right about there, do you believe it? It's in good shape too."

Jack looked at his watch. "We might make it to the ship in time to stop the ceremony." He led Margie toward the bench to collect her possessions.

"You know, if Brittany and Andrew are truly in love, this certificate won't stop them from marrying."

"I'm betting it will stop McDonald," Jack replied, grinning. "As a matter of fact, I'm counting on it."

Margie meant to return to the airport but Jack insisted she stay with him as they disembarked the ferry. They reached the cruise ship by eleven-thirty.

Allowed on board to attend the wedding, Jack rushed ahead of Margie. "Come on, come on," he urged from the foot of the highly polished staircase. A five thousand pound chandelier hung above his head.

"Elevator," Margie pointed out.

Jack hopped from the stairs, grabbed her arm, and raced for the hallway. "I knew I married you for a reason."

Rows of terraces lined the enormous foyer. Above her, Margie could see passengers moving along the edge of the walkways, entering rooms, and shutting doors. Some leaned over the railing to survey the atrium below.

The elevator doors stood open and Jack pulled Margie behind him. It was a tight squeeze when two men followed them inside. The tallest fellow wore a sling on his left arm. They pushed past Margie to stand behind her.

Margie whispered, "Do you think the ceremony has started?"

"It doesn't matter because I'll stop it."

"What will you do, fake a heart attack, pull the fire alarm to set off the sprinklers?"

Jack's brows knitted together. "I'm going to stand up and object."

"Oh," Margie accepted with an awkward glance. "Right, that's one way to do it."

The elevator door slid aside and Jack propelled Margie ahead of him. They rounded a corner, slipped down a narrow passageway, and then hurried onto the open deck. A large and beautiful swimming pool took up most of this level of the ship. Three slides towered above the water and rows of blue and white deck chairs formed perfectly straight lines at poolside. A cabana-style bar occupied the entire portside while a small group of people gathered near the stern for the wedding ceremony. Other passengers mingled in the late morning sunshine to drink coffee.

Brittany and Andrew faced the Atlantic Ocean as the captain of the ship stood in front of them. A photographer stepped to the side and raised his camera to snap a picture of the happy couple. He was a bushy mustached fellow in a Hawaiian shirt, beige shorts, navy socks, and penny loafers. A fishing hat fit over his brown curly hair. He stared at Margie and then winked.

Margie ignored him and watched the ceremony. Brittany wore a miniskirt made of white faille material with a tulle bustle knotted in an airy fashion. She looked slender and tanned with her rich dark hair tangled on top of her head in a charming hairdo.

Jack dropped Margie's hand and took large steps toward the couple. "I object," he announced, just like he swore he would do. "As brother of the bride I object to this wedding."

For some reason, this upset Brittany. "Jack," she cried spinning toward him.

Two waiters standing near Margie stared, astounded at the unexpected scene.

Andrew McDonald turned around quickly. He was very handsome with his chiseled features and full mouth. His pale blond hair fell in a layered style. Broad-shouldered and narrow-hipped, he confronted Jack. "Do you need another punch on the nose, Ivan?"

Margie took cover behind a tall pillar as the two waiters shot quick glances at each other.

Captain Norrell was a square-jawed man of about sixty and he looked neat and orderly in his white coat and slacks. "You can't object, young man." He flipped through the pages of his wedding manual. "We're not up to that point in the booklet."

Jack's voice remained resolute. He said, "I still object." He cocked his head at Andrew. "You might like to know something before you make any commitments this morning."

Andrew McDonald stood as tall as Jack and his cool eyes stabbed at him like ice daggers. "Oh really?" Andrew asked, his tone dripping with mockery. "And what would that be?"

"Margie and I were married last night."

Brittany's face sobered. One giant tear smeared her black eyeliner. She looked around the deck. "Who is Margie?"

"Who is Margie?" one waiter mouthed to the other.

Jack turned and pointed toward her.

"Hello," Margie called softly.

Andrew's head turned and his eyes narrowed coldly. "I don't believe you."

"Margie," Jack called, holding out his hand for the certificate. "I guess I'll just have to prove it to you."

Andrew McDonald's countenance darkened when Margie stepped forward while rummaging through her purse.

Suddenly, a pair of Bahamian men ran toward her and grabbed the bag out of her hand.

Chapter Seven

My ring!" cried Margie.

"My certificate!" Jack hollered at the same time.

The Bahamians were halfway down the passageway before anyone gave chase. Margie followed Jack and Andrew followed Margie. Brittany, with her veil lifted and her bustle bouncing, chased Andrew. A few wedding guests, Captain Norrell, and the waiters followed after Brittany.

Down the twisting staircase, the whole group descended in a wild free-for-all gallop. Jack would have gained on the purse snatchers had it not been for the parade of stair-climbing passengers returning from a late breakfast on Paradise Island.

The thieves skirted the catwalk toward the parking lot when everyone exploded onto the lowest deck. Jack pushed his way past travelers while holding onto the railing.

Margie paused on the landing and tried to find the

best route to the catwalk. That's when a thick fellow plowed into the back of her.

"Oof, sorry," the heavily mustached man muttered. He snapped a photo of Jack and Andrew racing down the gangway.

Margie narrowed her eyes. "What are you doing here?"

Holding the camera steady and pointing it at Margie, he asked, "Wouldn't you like a nice photograph of today's events?"

"Knock it off, Frierson, I recognize you." She shook her head at him. "By the way, your disguises have been slipshod this go-around. I spotted you at least ten times."

"You tore out of Tampa so fast that I didn't have time to arrange my wardrobe," Ernie Frierson countered. He snapped a picture of Margie shoving her way onto the walkway.

"I thought your name was Nelson!" Brittany hollered after Ernie.

He responded, "That's only what the name badge reads, darling."

Margie was halfway down the catwalk when she saw one of the thieves open the door of a beat up Cutlass Supreme that used to be blue. Only patches of the color clung to the sides of the auto now.

The other thief still held Margie's purse and jumped into the backseat through an open window.

Jack closed in on the Cutlass, running fast in his boots with his plaid shirt flapping at his sides. Andrew ran right behind him.

The car started with an enormous backfire and smoke mushroomed through half the parking lot. When Margie saw the Cutlass again, Jack was riding on its hood. He slid sideways when the car stalled two hundred yards later. Falling to the pavement, Jack grabbed the man's legs still dangling out the backseat window.

The car roared to life again just as Andrew drew even with Jack. Both of them slapped and punched at the man in the car who kicked and flailed and then delivered a swift kick to Andrew's jaw.

"Oh . . . oh, honey, are you okay?" Brittany wailed when her groom hit the blacktop and skidded backward on the tail of his suit jacket.

Jack still held on to the door handle as the car pulled away and then stalled again. Margie hollered encouragement. "Don't let them get away, Jack! That's a two-carat diamond ring!"

Brittany slid to a stop in her wedding pumps. "Jack gave you a two-carat diamond?"

"He had a little help from Tyler Bonaguide," Ernie Frierson said. He paused to snap another photo. "Isn't that right, Margie?"

Just then the driver of the Cutlass punched the gas pedal and the car leapt forward. This time the engine stuck. The car rattled away at fifteen miles-per-hour. Thick white smoke bloomed out the tailpipe.

Jack and Andrew sprinted after it as it clattered past the gate and into the street. The Cutlass took the corner and then gunned it to twenty miles-per-hour down Bay Street. Brittany stumbled to a stop next to Margie at the gate. Her dark brown hair slipped from the pretty, white flowered clips and fell into her face. She held her bridal pumps in one hand. "We'll never catch up," she said between gasps for air.

That was when Margie spied the two-wheeled cart outside the straw market. Of course it didn't have a decent animal attached to it like a horse or even a pony. There stood a donkey decked out in a straw hat that someone thought would be cute to stick on its head.

"I don't think this is a good idea," Frierson chimed in when Brittany climbed into the wagon and balanced on her knees at the front of it.

Margie found the donkey's reins. "I don't remember inviting you along."

"I'm just trying to make a living," he told her and snapped a photo of Margie, none too elegantly mounting the donkey stomach-first. Once up, she coaxed the animal forward.

The donkey ambled two steps to stand in traffic.

"Giddy-up," she shouted over the blasting car horns. "Giddy-up," Margie shouted again, but the donkey didn't budge. So, she yelled something Jack Ivan would holler at such a moment: "Giddy-up, you no-good, miserable glue factory candidate!" and then kicked the sides of the donkey with her canvas shoes.

The animal shot off like a stallion bursting out of the gate at the Kentucky Derby.

Margie's shoulders hit the rump of the donkey as it galloped away in fright. At first she stared at the blue sky waggling above her and then she got a tighter grip on the reins and pulled herself up into a sitting position again. Her ponytail came loose and her teeth chattered like finger cymbals.

The exploding scene pretty much brought the straw market to a standstill—until a pair of snarling dogs sprang out from a side street and barked at the cart and at the donkey. Tourists and vendors dove for cover. Umbrella tables overturned. Straw hats and dolls sailed skyward.

"Sorry," Margie hollered. "Excuse us, watch the donkey. Get out of the way!"

Jack and Andrew were just ahead of the two-wheeled cart now and still chasing the sputtering Cutlass. Margie and the donkey overtook Andrew first. "Jump on!" she called to him.

A dog bit his pant leg and Andrew kicked at it. Sweat streamed down his rangy features and into his thick-lashed eyes. When he slowed to make a jump for the cart, Brittany slapped him on the head.

"Oww," he complained, still fighting off one of the dogs. He ducked in time to avoid Brittany's next swipe.

She wailed, "You left me at the altar!"

"I thought you would want me to help your brother." He made another attempt to board the wagon.

"Help him do what, stop our wedding?" Her next swing went wild and she nearly fell out of the cart.

One of the wheels hit a rock in the road and began to wobble as splinters of wood shot out on either side of the cart. The dogs broke away for a moment. It gave Andrew the opportunity to jump into the wagon. Flames sparked when the back of the cart dragged along the ground with the added weight. The other wheel started to fragment when the donkey crested a hill and then started the descent. The cart boards strained against their nails.

The donkey drew even with Jack. When position allowed, Brittany cuffed him too. The dogs darted toward Jack and leapt at him. He took a quick kick at one of the beasts.

Margie tried to help by lashing out with her foot. Jack elbowed the next dog and kept running. Brittany threw a wedding pump into the mix.

The Cutlass pulled over and parked on the side of the road. Perhaps the thieves thought they'd lost their pursuers but they were wrong. Their pursuers gained on them, caught up with them, and then passed them on an exploding donkey cart.

Brittany and Andrew and Ernie Frierson sprang from the wagon just as the cart self-destructed. There was nothing left of the two-wheeler but a streak of rubble stretching from the top of the hill to the bottom.

Margie dismounted the donkey and ran toward Jack, who stood and brushed off his jeans. His damp hair fell across his forehead. He wiped his face and straightened his shirt onto his shoulders again.

Most of the vendors and customers in the market gaped at the remains of the two-wheeler. Some walked cautiously toward it. Margie could see Brittany and Andrew and Ernie Frierson further up the street, wiping their clothes and pulling wood splinters from their hair.

"Come on," Jack said, hurrying her along. Margie

followed him through a narrow and dark passage. Most people ran toward the crash scene so the alley seemed deserted. A child cried behind a door. Someone's laundry hung off a fire escape.

A peculiar odor filled the tightening space when Jack and Margie slipped around a corner. At the end of the alley, a door banged shut. The sign above the door read TOHO'S CREMATORIUM.

"Do you think it was them?" she asked, following Jack toward the door.

He pulled on the knob. "There's one way to find out."

This was the back door to the business and Margie moved closer to Jack. "What will we do when we catch them?"

"What will we do?" he scoffed. "We'll take back the purse."

"What if they have weapons?"

"Yeah . . ." Jack hesitated. "Maybe you should go first." He grinned down at her in the semi-darkness, as if he thoroughly enjoyed this.

They stepped into a narrow hallway. A slender table sat along one wall and a small lamp cast a soft light. Jack tried one door but it was locked.

Margie didn't like this one bit. Chasing thieves in the open daylight was one thing but tiptoeing through a crematorium was quite another. They could easily stumble upon something . . . lifeless. Think happy thoughts, she told herself. Think fields of flowers and sunset walks along the beach. Think tranquil composed ruminations.

And who or what was panting so loudly!?

Margie took a hold of herself. She was the one pant-ing. She closed her mouth and tried taking deep, medi-tative breaths through her nose.

"What is that sound?" Jack asked beside her.

"I'm breathing."

"You sound like you're sucking wind from an oxy-gen mask."

Ho-ho, he was a funny man, a funny man in a crema-torium.

Jack tried another door and this time it opened. Margie went halfway into the room when he flipped on the light switch. The bright light revealed a naked man—probably ten years older than Methuselah—lying in state on a cold metal table. Margie's eyes popped wide. A shudder con-vulsed her body.

"Oh . . . my . . . word!" she screeched. Then she ran for the door. Jack tried to squeeze out at the same time, which meant they were caught together in the door jam. The harder they pushed the more difficult it became to breathe. Nearly to their knees, Margie felt something on her calf. "Something's got my leg. Something's got my leeeeg!"

Jack bore down hard and finally fell out of the door. "It's your Wal-Mart bag," he told her in disgust.

"Oh," Margie said, composed now, and pulled at the plastic. Bag in hand, she stepped over Jack, and waited for him to stand. When he did, he shut the door and tried the next.

Nothing. The room was empty. "Come on," he mut-tered and moved carefully down the hall.

Voices sounded muffled behind a new door. Light seeped beneath it. Jack took a steady breath, and with the intention of surprising the thieves, shouldered the door open. He burst into the room with a great, "Hand it over now!"

An old woman acknowledged his presence with a scream and the younger woman standing next to the old lady threw her purse at him. Jack threw it back, and without a word, slammed the door with a mighty thud.

Margie couldn't help it. A snort escaped before the giggles erupted. She fell against the wall and weakly leaned toward Jack.

He glared at her. Obviously he was embarrassed. And he should be embarrassed. He had just held up two little unarmed ladies. It was horrible behavior. Really.

He stormed ahead of her into what looked like a reception area. Simple sheers covered the windows facing Bay Street. A velour couch sat along one wall and two wingback chairs faced the sofa. Jack silently pointed to a door behind the reception counter.

Without warning, the door opened.

Jack dove for cover behind the counter.

Margie went into a crouch too and then waddled toward a plastic tree to melt into the scenery of the room. She was a thin girl but she couldn't quite hide behind the slender trunk of a ficus, so when the three men who emerged from the room weren't looking, she did a rapid crawl toward one of the wingback chairs.

The men spoke broken English as they rounded the counter.

Jack tackled the first man he saw.

The man cursed as he fell to the floor.

Margie jumped up from behind the chair and grabbed her purse from the second man rounding the corner.

He grabbed it in return.

She grabbed it again and turned to run, but Jack and his tumbling partner knocked her at the knees, and she fell right on top of them.

About that time, the third man stepped around their thrashing figures and pulled the purse from the tussle.

"Children in the school yard," he declared with great authority. Margie presumed this was Toho, the owner of this establishment. He towered above them sprawled there on the floor. "Rise up and straighten your clothing." He said this with a slight British accent that made him sound very formal.

Everyone did as he said. And no one wondered why, except Margie, who realized she was taller than Toho when she stood. And, now that she got a good look at the older man, she accused, "I know you; you're the fellow who married us last night."

"KengrUtleleilen I—tju" Toho answered. "Congratulations."

He leaned against the reception counter and Margie noticed something else. Her engagement ring was on his pinkie finger. She pointed at the diamond. "I'm going to need that ring back."

Toho studied the diamond, wiggled his finger, and

then smiled at her. "It was a recent gift to me. I cannot give it to you."

Jack stepped forward. "Keep the diamond, pal. All we want is the purse."

Margie frowned at him. "They can keep the purse. I need my ring. Tyler will kill me if I come home without it." She faced Toho again. "My fiancé is a very important lawyer in the States."

"I thought you said you were married."

"You know," Jack rounded on him, "I wish you would've spoken English last night during our little ceremony on Little Abaco."

"People want drama," he explained with a shrug. Then he looked at Margie again. "So, your fiancé is a . . ."

"Lawyer," she finished for him. "Did you ever hear of Tyler Bonaguide, hmm? And when Tyler finds out about this robbery you've pulled off, he'll take you to court. He'll take everything you've got while he's at it. Say good-bye to your little wedding business and your little crematorium here."

"Can he get me a visa?"

Margie's brow went up. "You want a visa?"

"I've tried to get one and have been denied because of my less than perfect criminal record."

"No kidding?" asked Jack.

The old man waved his hand. "Let's go see your lawyer and I will return your ring and your purse to you."

Margie paused. "He lives in Florida."

"I've got a better idea," Jack told the old man. "How about I call the police and we take the ring and the purse without anyone going anywhere?"

That's when the two women whom Jack had startled came into the room and pointed at him. "He tried to steal my purse," the younger woman accused. Toho raised a brow at Jack.

Jack said, "What were you saying about a visa?"

"Bring your lawyer to me," Toho told Margie. He waggled the ring again causing the 100-facet stone to sparkle wildly. "Bring him to the spot where it all began."

Jack screwed up his face in confusion. "What spot would that be?"

"He means Little Abaco," Margie explained. "Get it? The place where it all began. You and I began there." She looked at Toho again. "That is what you mean, isn't it? Or do you mean the police station where your men first saw my ring?"

Jack scowled at her. "He doesn't mean the police station, for crying out loud."

Toho closed his eyes, held up his hand, and shook his head. "I mean the island. Bring the lawyer before tonight's ceremony."

"I feel like we accomplished our goal," Margie told Jack, following him out of the alley and into the bright sunshine.

Glancing over his shoulder, he grumbled, "What goal? We didn't get the diamond or the certificate." He stepped onto the sidewalk. "All you managed to retrieve was your cell phone, which appears to be broken."

She paused for reflection and then brightened. "We accomplished the goal of not seeing one more naked dead man."

"Oh yeah," came his derisive comment. "That was on my to-do list."

Angry voices caused Margie to glance northward at the gathered crowd. Three policemen tried to pull a wailing donkey out of the middle of the road. Andrew and Brittany quarreled nearby. Brittany hollered something over the top of a vendor woman's head and then threw her remaining wedding pump at Andrew. Andrew ducked and the pump hit Officer Peety in the back of the head. Officer Peety promptly pulled out his cuffs.

Margie steered southward, appreciating the fact that domestic disturbances could be left—and should be left—to the authorities.

"Where do you think you're going?" Jack asked her, catching up.

"I need to find a pay phone, but I have no cash because I no longer have my purse." She shook her cellular phone and pointed the antenna toward the west. "I know this isn't completely dead. It worked . . ."

"Put it away. I have an idea."

Margie had an idea too.

Jack said, "Why don't we—"

"The hotel," Margie interjected.

"What?"

"The hotel . . . my phone worked at the Radisson last

night. I know because Tyler called me at two o'clock in the morning."

Jack stopped mid-step. "You were at the Radisson last night?"

"Why are you just standing there? Let's find a taxi or a donkey or something."

Margie held her cell phone out in front of her, turned right, turned left, and still got no transmission. "This is crazy."

"Can I help you?" an older gentleman asked Jack, who leaned on the reservation desk.

When the man cleared his throat, Jack glanced over his shoulder. "Oh," he said, spinning around. "Good afternoon."

The clerk wasn't looking at Jack. He explained, "She can't twirl like that in our lobby."

"Really?" he asked, taking in the beautiful room. Rich furniture filled the lobby and sat upon a Persian rug. Polished wood sparkled beneath a very large chandelier.

"Really," the gentleman replied. "She'll have to twirl outside."

Jack realized the hotel guests were starting to stare at Margie so he asked, "If I book a room, does she get to twirl?"

"What you do behind closed doors is your business, sir."

Jack shrugged and slapped the counter. "Then give me a room."

* * *

Off the elevator, Margie followed Jack to their room. When he slipped the key into the lock, she wondered aloud, "Three sixteen again?" Walking into the room, she missed Jack's confused look at the door and its brass numbers.

Stepping into the room, he shut the door and told her, "Will you put the cell phone away?"

"Right," she agreed and tossed it on the bed. "I can use the phone on the nightstand." She set her Wal-Mart bag on the floor, sat on the mattress, and reached for the receiver.

Jack stopped her by tapping his finger on the button. He hunkered down in front of her, took the receiver, and replaced it in the cradle. "Listen to me for a minute."

He caught and held her gaze. His gold crucifix glinted in the sunshine that streamed through the tall window directly behind him. His dark hair waved loosely atop his head and curled at his ears. Dark lashes nearly touched as he squinted. "I don't want you to call Tyler." He took Margie's fingers in both his hands and leaned forward slightly. He completely held her attention now.

"I have to call Tyler. How else will we get a visa for Toho?"

"No," he told her, pursing his mouth. He shook his head. "Forget the visa. Forget Toho."

"But, your certificate . . ."

"Margie," he uttered fervently. "Let's get married."

Her breath stopped. "What?"

"Marry me. Marry me this afternoon."

Margie's lips parted but she couldn't find a word to

answer his proposal. Did Jack love her? Did he admit it now, down on his knees, and so desperately searching for an answer with his very dark brown eyes?

He shifted his weight and sat next to her on the bed. "We can run down the street to the little wedding chapel I passed this morning when I searched for you."

"Jack," she whispered. "Are you serious?" Margie longed to hear him say he loved her. Her eyes settled on his full mouth and she waited for him to kiss her.

He leaned in and with his lips only a breath away, he asserted, "It's the only way, Margie, don't you see? As soon as we get to the States, we'll get the marriage annulled. I'll disappear after that. You won't ever have to see me again and I'll never ask you for another thing." His arm went around her shoulders. "Come on, Margie. Do this last thing for me."

The phone rang.

Margie tried to stand and reach the receiver but Jack pulled her back onto the bed.

The phone rang again and then again until frustrated, Jack reached for it and slammed the earpiece into the cradle.

He chose the wrong phone.

With shaky hands, Margie reached for her cell phone. This was her wake-up call. What was she allowing? Would she really have given in to Jack's proposal?

Yes, because when he pleaded with her everything seemed logical and justified. Margie loved Jack and she wanted to help him—but marry him *knowingly*, that was different. She was engaged! Tyler would find out, or his political opponents would.

The phone in her hand rang a fourth time just as Jack sat on the bed again. She mashed the talk button on the cell phone. "Hello?"

"Margie?" her fiancé asked. Something in her voice must have caused him concern. "What's wrong?"

"Tyler? Can you come?"

Jack's head snapped up and his dark brow formed one long frown. He reached for the cell phone. "Margie," he hissed quietly.

Tyler asked, "Are you still in the Bahamas?"

"Yes." She closed her eyes so she couldn't see Jack's angry expression; she opened them again when the mattress bounced and Jack shot off the bed.

"I'm checking the Internet for a flight," Tyler told her. "Tell me what's wrong."

"I'll tell you everything when you get here. Please hurry."

Jack circled the bed and then sat on the edge of it.

She swallowed hard and waited.

"There's a four o'clock flight out of Tampa. I'll be there by five. Will you be at the airport?"

Jack's eyes held hers. His jaw squared and a muscle worked as he ground his teeth hard. His nostrils flared in anger.

"Margie?" Tyler asked. "Will you be there?"

"Yes," she told him breathlessly and pressed the end button.

"Why did you do that?" Jack demanded.

A cold chill washed over her at the tone of his voice. "We need Tyler."

"No, we don't." Jack pushed to his feet and stormed around the room. His fists jammed onto his hips. "I don't. I can settle this without your baby-kissing, hand-shaking lawyer."

Margie sat up on the bed. "I have to have the diamond, Jack." She pushed the hair out of her face. "What would I tell Tyler if I didn't have his ring?"

"What are you going to tell him anyway?" Jack asked, throwing out his hands and leaning toward her. "How are you going to explain the way you lost it in the first place?"

"I intend to tell Tyler the truth, that my ring was stolen."

Jack crouched down next to the bed. "Are you going to tell him that you're my wife?" His voice was as much a caress as his hand would be and he tilted his head to catch her eyes. "Margie, forget the diamond. Tell Tyler you lost it and buy him a new ring if he insists on it. You've got the means, but I'm out of resources. Money can't help me. Only you can."

"I'm not going to marry you," whispered Margie, swallowing hard and looking at her fingers instead of his dark pleading eyes.

"You're not going to help me?"

Heart clenching, she shook her head. "I can't . . ."

Jack's sharp intake of breath caused her to look at him. He spun away from her and placed his hands on the dresser.

Then he turned back to lean there and crossed his arms over his chest. Angry again, he accused, "You don't even make sense, Margie." His breathing grew rapid and his jaw worked before he questioned, "What do you do, tag along only while the fun lasts? But when things turn serious, when the odds are stacked so hugely against a man, you decide to call in Bonaguide?"

"No . . ." she answered miserably, standing now and longing to explain her doubts to him.

"How many times has the poor man bailed you out?"

She dropped her hands to her sides with the accusation.

"Answer me," he said in a voice with just a hint of menace lurking in it. "Are you the bored little rich girl?" His hand reached out and he pulled her chin up. "Can't your money buy enough thrills? Do you always have to cross the line just to see where you'll end up?"

She pulled her face away. "That's not true."

"Really?" he asked, leaning toward her. "I think it is. This has been a good time for you and all I am is a diversion and a break from your dull routine. A marriage certificate is life and death to me, Margie, but to you, it's a souvenir."

"No, that's . . ." she began but Jack turned away from her and picked up the key from the top of the dresser. "Where are you going?"

He reached for the doorknob. "Go find your beloved Tyler. I will help myself from here on out."

Margie followed him anyway because she doubted Jack had a clue of what to do next. She didn't realize she still held her cell phone in her hand until it rang inside the elevator.

Cat was on the other end. "What's going on, Margie? Uncle Bonny just called and asked for Dad's phone number in Maryland."

So, Tyler had called in the cavalry.

"He wouldn't tell me what happened," Cat continued. "All he said was, 'your sister is at it again.' "

Margie glanced at Jack, who ignored her and stared at the button panel on the wall. When the elevator doors opened, she followed him into the lobby. To Cat, she explained, "I haven't told Tyler everything yet, but my ring was stolen, and my purse was stolen, and I'm being blackmailed . . . Well, the list just goes on and on, but let me explain it to him, all right?"

"You're not injured or in jail or about to be offered as a burnt sacrifice?"

"Give me the rest of the day," Margie told her and then jogged after Jack, who nearly sprinted to the sidewalk and headed toward the ferry service.

Chapter Eight

Jack knocked on the Civic Hall window and a small woman of about sixty slid the glass aside. Margie recognized her. She was the receptionist at last night's wedding ceremony.

This was a good sign, or so Jack seemed to think. Perhaps the woman remembered them. He nodded encouragingly at Margie and then explained, "We were married here last night and we've lost our certificate. We would like a copy."

The woman smiled brightly. "Come back this evening. There will be another ceremony."

Jack shifted his weight. "Well, that's just it. I can't come back this evening," he explained. "I'm leaving and I need a copy—"

"No copies," the woman interrupted, holding up her hand. "No copies. We have one original and we give it to the bride and groom. Come back this evening."

"I just said that I can't . . ."

The woman looked a little hysterical. "I said *no copies.*"

Jack left the window and walked toward the parking lot. When Margie caught up with him, she offered, "We'll get my purse back, Jack. It will be all right."

"I don't believe we're going to get your purse back, Margie." He walked without looking at her.

This attitude was so unlike Jack. He never gave up this easily. Why wasn't he busting up the Civic Hall to pull a certificate out of someone's armpit? Margie soothed, "Sure we will, you'll see. Tyler is quite the negotiator. My family has retained his services for years." They reached the path and pushed past the hibiscus bushes. "But listen, Jack. You can't tell him we're married."

Jack spun to look at her then. "Really, Margie? You want me to lie for you?"

"You don't have to lie. Just don't mention the marriage bit."

The sun showed red streaks running through his long dark hair. His jaw squared and an angry look crossed his features. "Okay, Margie. I won't tell because I'm just so happy for you. You can wreak havoc all you like and he'll run to your rescue. It's a perfect fairy-tale life. I hope you'll be happy together."

Margie winced at him, ready to argue, but her cell phone rang and Margie said, "Hey," after she checked the display that read *Cat.*

"We're on our way."

Margie glanced at Jack, who had his arm in the air to

hail a cab. She asked, "Why are you on the way?" Not that she complained. She needed her family now more than ever.

"I booked the same flight as Tyler and Uncle Bonny. We'll be there at five. Dad couldn't get a flight until later and won't arrive until six thirty."

"Terrific," Margie said with as much enthusiasm as she could muster. "I'll meet you there." When she rang off, Margie looked at Jack. "Where are you going now?"

"To the airport."

It took them nearly an hour and a half to get off the island because they missed one ferry and had to wait for the next.

The weather turned gloomy and a mist of fine raindrops moistened Margie's hair completely. There was little cover on the ferry. The clouds matched her mood anyway, so she might as well look like a mop. She brushed the damp locks off her forehead and stared at Jack. He stood with his back to her and gazed at the water. He had been mad before, sure, but never like this. But, if he would just stop for a minute and think about what he had asked her to do . . .

Margie felt badly for him. But hadn't she already helped him as much as she possibly could? She couldn't marry Jack. It would spell political disaster for Tyler.

Besides, Jack didn't love her. He'd never said he did. He *needed* her but he didn't seem to *care* about her. Margie could never marry anyone who didn't love her.

Her head snapped up and she straightened her shoulders. She couldn't marry Tyler for the same reason she couldn't marry Jack. How could she? Margie didn't love Tyler and never would love him. Tyler didn't love her either.

She stood with the realization. She would not marry Tyler Bonaguide! How exhilarating. How freeing. And when she recovered his ridiculously oversized engagement ring, she would give it back to him with a swift handshake and a firm good-bye.

Oh, she'd lose her inheritance until she was thirty, but Margie didn't care now. She still got a decent allowance and could easily make due with that. And when the man she loved swore he couldn't live a day without her, then Margie would marry; only then and with great enthusiasm. She would plan a wedding with panache and flair and there would be no Italian or Swiss buttercream icing allowed in a five-mile radius.

It was too bad Jack wouldn't be the groom on that special day. Margie sank into her chair again. Suddenly, she had an overwhelming desire to return to that little out-island near Andros and live stranded for the rest of her days. It was more sufferable than having Jack so angry with her.

Jack walked with head held high into the Bahamas Air terminal. Wasn't he a rooster, all wounded and hurting but strutting regardless? Margie waited while he bought a ticket to Tampa and then slid the travel document into his shirt pocket. She glanced at her bangle wristwatch. It read 4:55.

When Jack stepped out of line, Margie asked him, "Are you sure you don't want to stick around and try to recover your certificate?"

He didn't look at her but at the magazine rack nearby. "Yeah, I'm sure."

She nodded. "Well, if I find it, I'll mail it to you." She tried to catch his eye. "The Flying D, right?"

"For the time being." He glanced at her and pulled the ticket out of his pocket to study it. "In a couple of months it will be absorbed into the Bar M Ranch."

Margie wanted to grab him by the shoulders and shake him. She wanted to holler. *Will you snap out of it?* But she didn't. Tyler Bonaguide would walk through the gate any minute now and quality alone time with Jack would be lost forever.

Margie desperately wanted Jack to say something, anything, to her. If he would just acknowledge they had had an adventure together, that he liked her just a little, and that he might possibly miss her when she was gone. She tried to prompt him by asking, "What time does your flight leave?"

"In twenty minutes." He still didn't look at her, only out the huge windows, and the tarmac beyond.

"So, this is really good-bye," she prompted once more.

"Yeah."

Margie exhaled in frustration "Well . . . good-bye," she said, angry now.

Jack's face reddened. "What are you mad about?"

"Well, what do you think?" She had already turned to walk away but spun around to frown at him. "We're parting ways here, Jack; doesn't that mean something to you? Aren't you going to say anything to me at all?"

Jack took a step in her direction with a sincere look of confusion on his face. His dark eyes narrowed and he shook his head slightly. "Something . . . like what?" He took another step. "What do you want, a thank you?"

All the anger went out of her and her throat tightened in grief. "I don't want your thanks. My life is just as screwed up as yours, you know?"

He seemed to think about it for a moment. "You're truly worried about what Tyler is going to say about all of this? That just shocks me, Margie." He raked dark hair out of his face and his eyebrows came together. He stood directly in front of her now, looking down at her with those black-lashed eyes. "This whole time we've spent together, you never acted engaged. You never acted worried about what Tyler Bonaguide thought about you tearing off to the islands. You acted like—"

"Believe it or not, Jack, this was the first time I've ever torn off anywhere."

"You acted like you cared about what was happening to me. You stuck with me when I tried to find Brittany and when I tried to stop the wedding." He threw his arms out wide and then slapped his chest with one hand. "I thought I meant something to you and I really thought you would help me."

"I can't marry—"

"I'm not asking you again!" This last bit was shouted at about two million decibels and pretty much brought the terminal to hushed silence. Jack looked left and right and then exhaled. "I know what your answer is, Margie. You prefer Tyler. You need Tyler . . ."

"I do not prefer Tyler!"

People in the line forming next to the gate glanced uneasily at each other. Margie tried to lower her voice. Afraid she would start to cry, she clamped down hard on her teeth. After a deep breath, she said in a more composed voice, "The least you could've done while asking me to marry you is act as though you cared about me."

The stunned look on Jack's face would've been comical if she wasn't so upset and angry with him. He asked, "You think I don't care about you?"

"You *need* me, Jack. I know that. Why don't you go back to your boring lifestyle?"

"Wait a minute—"

"Margie?" Tyler's voice called out above Jack's.

She twisted around to see Tyler and Uncle Bonny standing behind her. "Hi," she offered weakly. Tyler still wore a crisp white shirt and gray trousers, like he had just left his office in Tampa. His dark hair lay perfectly in place as his green eyes shifted from Margie to Jack.

"What's going on here?"

Margie quickly hugged him, though he didn't return the affection. He kept his jacket over one arm and his briefcase in the other hand. He felt stiff and unyielding and his eyes never left Jack.

"Well, here we are," Morris Bonaguide announced, oblivious to the tension between Tyler and Margie and Jack. "What's the emergency?"

It was nice to see him too.

Uncle Bonny's blue gaze held Margie's. "What sort of international trouble have you caused: social anarchy, the fall of the Bahamian government?" He paused then and looked beyond Margie's shoulder. "And you, what are you doing here?"

Jack smiled at Morris Bonaguide. The fact that he still stood there surprised Margie because she thought Jack would've joined the travelers in line. She steadied her breathing. "Um, Tyler . . . this is Jack Ivan."

Jack stuck out his hand and Tyler hesitantly took it.

"He's leaving in fifteen minutes."

"I'm not leaving," Jack said in a matter-of-fact tone while pumping Tyler's hand.

Margie frowned at him. "You're not?"

"No." He wore an odd smile on his face.

"I thought . . ." Margie started.

"I changed my mind," Jack told her, finally glancing at her, and then back to Tyler.

Morris Bonaguide repeated, "What are you doing here?"

"My sister is here. You remember my sister, Brittany? She used to work for you."

Morris nodded. "Brittany Ivan?"

"Yes."

"She's here?"

"That's what I just said." Jack still wore that clever

little grin, like he had one up on everybody in the airport.

Margie wrinkled her nose at him. What was he up to now?

"Margie," called Cat from the gate, and Margie spun around to see her sister emerge from the gate door. She had three times the hair of the average woman and she wore it in a ponytail that hung down her back in ringlets. Cat reached for her and when she was close enough, she hugged Margie fiercely. "What is going on around here?"

"I'll explain in a minute. Cat, this is Jack Ivan. Jack, this is my sister Cat."

Jack's grin broadened into a genuine smile. "Hello," he said very pleasantly. He sounded happy to meet her.

What was wrong with him?

But the time had come to explain. Since everyone stood expectant in a circle around her, Margie announced, "My purse and my engagement ring were stolen."

"What?" Tyler asked, finally taking his eyes off Jack.

Uncle Bonny stuttered, "Were your credit cards and bank information in your purse?"

Before she could answer, Tyler wanted to know, "Have you contacted the police?"

And that was a very good question.

"No," Margie began. "The police would take too long to recover my belongings, so we, Jack and I, caught up to the fellows ourselves and struck a deal."

Tyler and Uncle Bonnie leaned forward with raised brows.

Cat winced as if she expected a painful blow at any second.

Margie rushed her words, "Toho-will-give-the-ring-back-to-me-if-you-arrange-a-visa-to-the-U.S."

Tyler blinked at her. "Excuse me?"

"He wants a visa."

Tyler stared at his father who stared at him in return.

Cat stared at Margie and then at Jack.

Margie stared at everyone and then at Jack, who apparently thought the whole scene was some sort of slapstick comedy. His eyes looked bright and they crinkled at the corners. A half smile played across his mouth.

"No," Tyler said in an angry voice. "No deal. We're going to the police."

Margie stopped him by placing a hand on his arm. "I didn't think you would want all the publicity over this, Tyler."

He leaned in toward her and hissed, "I don't. This is just great, Margie." His eyes were chips of green ice. "But I'm not going to be swept into the whirlpool of one of your catastrophes."

She admitted the worst of it then. "He knows your name."

"How does he know Tyler's name?" Morris asked.

"Well, I-I mentioned it during the negotiation stage."

Tyler closed his eyes. "I see. So now someone can get a hold of this information?"

"I just thought you should know everything," she said, grimacing with the admission.

Tyler's features went rigid. "Where is he?"

"Little Abaco. It's an island just north of here."

"All right," Tyler said, turning toward his father, who still stared at Margie. "Let's check into a hotel and then I'll go with Margie."

"Right," Uncle Bonny agreed. "I'll come back to meet her father at six-thirty."

At the Radisson's reception desk, Tyler and Uncle Bonnie booked a room, as did Cat. The clerk asked, "Would you like rooms near the Ivans?"

Jack snorted a laugh and Margie drew their attention away. "It doesn't matter. We don't need rooms next to each other. We're one big quarreling family."

Ha ha.

Jack didn't see him coming, but Andrew McDonald stepped off the elevator, walked up behind him, and tapped him on the shoulder. "I just bailed your sister out of jail, Jack. I hope you're happy."

Jack straightened to square off with Andrew. "What was Brittany doing in jail?"

"After the donkey cart accident she threw her shoe at an officer of the law."

"Donkey cart accident?" Cat squinted her eyes with the question.

"I'll tell you later," Margie said with a rueful grin.

Andrew's blond hair looked messy on top of his head and a sliver of wood was still entangled near the back of it. "We also missed our boat's departure time and have to fly out tomorrow morning to catch up with our party on the next island."

"My heart's breaking for you, McDonald," Jack told him and winked at Margie. "Where is Brittany now?"

"Upstairs resting. She has a migraine. It was brought on by her allergies to the dogs."

Cat raised an eyebrow. "Dogs?" she asked Margie.

"I'll tell you later."

Andrew moved away but then remembered something. "I never did get to see that certificate you claim you have, Jack."

"I don't have it on me right now," Jack said gamely, feeling his shirt pocket as if he forgot where he put it.

Andrew nodded and then walked toward the pharmacy.

Cat said, "Well, I can't wait to hear all the amusing details of this trip." Her brown eyes twinkled behind very thick lashes. "I think you've outdone yourself this time."

"You won't believe it," Margie told her.

"Sure I will. I grew up with you. There's nothing possible or impossible that I won't believe."

Margie grinned at her. "Wait until I tell you about the naked dead guy."

Cat's face fell. "Okay, maybe I was wrong."

Jack leaned on the counter next to Margie again and she turned on him.

"What are you doing?" she whispered.

His eyebrows lifted. "I'm just standing here." He was trying to sound surprised at her question.

Margie knew better. "Why?"

"You want me to stand somewhere else?"

"No. Why aren't you leaving?"

Jack leaned forward and divulged, "I've decided it is in my best interest to stick around a little longer." He wiggled those brows at her as if he thought he was being very clever.

He was not clever. Margie knew exactly what he was doing and why he was staying. "Now that you've met Tyler, you think you have a chance of getting your certificate, is that it?"

"Actually, Bonaguide doesn't impress me much." He smiled brightly at her and then pushed off the desk when Tyler and Uncle Bonny stepped away from the counter.

"All right," Tyler said. "Let's go get this over with."

It was the fourth time Margie boarded the ferry to Little Abaco. This time she stood next to Tyler. Cat sat in a nearby deck chair and Jack sat alone. His eyes never left Margie as he sat sprawled out in a seat with his elbow on the armrest and his thumb massaging his bottom lip.

Tyler said something and Margie tried to focus on him. His brown hair tossed in the sea breeze and his eyes narrowed as he stared at Jack. "Explain to me what's going on here."

"I told you, my ring was stolen." Her eyes went from Tyler to Jack, then to Tyler again. "Maybe I should start at the beginning."

Tyler rubbed his forehead and finally looked at Margie. "All I want to know is why you're with him." He nodded toward Jack. "Why is he tagging along?"

"I carried a document of his in my purse and he wants it back."

"Why was his document in your purse?"

"So it wouldn't fall into the sand again. We had already lost it once on Little Abaco."

Tyler faced her square on. He said, "Explain to the court why you visited Little Abaco?" Actually, he only asked why she had been on the island in the first place, but the way his green eyes pierced hers, it seemed he was asking something else.

Margie clarified, "There was a luau, and after Jack threatened to take his own life, I put the document in my bag."

Tyler's head spun around to see Jack and then turned back to Margie. He whispered, "He's suicidal?"

"Gee, I don't know." She studied Jack too. He didn't look about to end his life by jumping off the ship. He looked pretty happy, as a matter of fact.

"You just said he threatened to take his life."

"Sure, because he was upset about the plane crash and the riot."

Tyler pushed off the railing and stood to his full height. "Plane crash?"

"Emergency landing, really. Anyway, I put the document in my Wal-Mart bag."

He shook his head in disbelief. "Since when do you shop at Wal-Mart?"

"Since my car broke down."

"The Jag broke down?"

He looked so concerned that Margie quickly explained, "It was only the battery. I should have listened to the mechanic who plugged the tire."

"You had a flat tire?"

Margie nodded. "Blowout. Jack didn't look where he was going."

"Jack was driving?"

"Ever since the gas station, yes, and don't ever use a restroom at a gas station, by the way."

After a judicious pause, Tyler asked, "When exactly did you meet Jack?" Tyler looked a little suicidal himself now.

Margie thought for a moment. "The first or second time?"

"Never mind," Tyler told her, holding up a hand to stop her flow of words. He watched the ocean and Margie bit her lip to stop a grin from forming on her lips. It wasn't every day she out-double-talked Tyler Norton Bonaguide, Esquire.

There were still two hours of daylight when Margie's party of four walked the stone path toward the beach. Workers lit tiki torches in anticipation of nightfall and of the next luau. Somewhere a pig squealed and Margie grimaced at Jack. Jack took the lead toward the Civic Hall. He tapped on the window as the rest of their group pressed forward to see the clerk open the glass. A small Bahamian man smiled at them all and said, "We are closed."

He meant to slide the window shut but Jack stuck his hand on the track. "We're looking for a man who performs the weddings here. His name is Toho."

"Toto?" Tyler asked Margie.

"Toho," she corrected.

The clerk bobbed his head happily. "Toho. He arrives at nightfall when the Hupa ceremony begins."

Tyler stepped forward. "What time does the ceremony begin?" He spoke slowly and with precise pronunciation as though the man did not understand plain English.

"When Toho arrives," the clerk answered in plain English.

"And when does he arrive?"

"When the ceremony begins."

"Okay, now we're getting somewhere," Margie declared.

Jack's smile broadened. "Does Toho live around here somewhere? He asked us to meet him before the ceremony."

Tyler mumbled, "He's not going to tell us where the guy lives."

The fellow pointed past Jack's shoulder. "Take the path and follow it over the bridge."

They walked toward the edge of the woods. The sky still looked overcast and the scent of rain floated on the breeze. Little Abaco's residents consisted mostly of donkeys, goats, and rare birds. Wild flamingos called to each other through the brush. A small goat passed in front of them when they stepped onto the rough path.

Tyler tripped over an exposed root and in a fit of

temper cried out, "What are we doing, what are we doing?" This was from the man who had most of his fun loitering in libraries and reading law books. "This is ludicrous. We're letting Toto drag us out here into his neighborhood."

"It's Toho," Margie corrected again.

"Whatever, we're walking into his world, his . . ."—he looked at their surroundings, the trees, the vines, the same goat chewing a leaf on the next bush over—"world of criminals and drug dealings and money laundering."

"If you're scared, Lawyer Boy, go to the beach and we'll bring Toho to you," Jack told him, walking back to stand in front of him.

"Lawyer Boy?"

Margie stepped between them. "He doesn't mean anything by it." She looked over her shoulder to give Jack a scorching look. Keeping her tone even, she explained, "He's hot-tempered."

"Yeah," Jack agreed, stepping closer. "I'm hot-tempered. You never know when I'll go off."

Tyler looked him over in a quick sweep. Jack was taller by two inches and broader by three. He said, in a more civil manner, "I just don't like the circumstances. I'm not going to be anyone's *corpus delicti*."

Jack's eyes narrowed. "Excuse me?"

"Murder victim," Tyler explained. "It's Latin for the body of the crime, such as the corpse of a murder victim or the charred frame of a torched building."

"Yeah, spellbinding," Jack replied, ready to walk on

again. "But we weren't dictating the arrangements. Two of the thieves carried knives."

"They threatened you?" he asked Margie. Would he defend her at last? Was there shining armor beneath his blazing white shirt? "I didn't think they would have weapons."

"You're a lawyer and you don't know criminal behavior?" asked Cat. Her curly dark hair fanned out on either side of her tanned face.

They walked the path again. Margie followed Jack and Cat followed her. Now Tyler brought up the rear. They walked another ten minutes until Jack stopped in a clearing. A narrow bridge crossed a twenty-foot by eight-foot gulch. He stepped on the decaying wood to test it and then crossed first.

Margie crossed next and while they waited on the opposite bank for Cat and Tyler, she asked Jack, "Why don't you like Tyler?"

"What?" He grabbed his chest in a shocked manner. "I like Tyler. He's great, just like you said. A little more simpering than you described, but I like him fine."

"Why are you being so hateful?"

He grinned at her and leaned close, as though he intended to kiss her. Margie's heart skipped a beat when he brought his face inches from hers. His dark eyes locked on Margie's. "Because I'm hot-blooded and I can't help myself."

"I said you are hot-*tempered*."

He grinned, flashing white teeth. "Yeah, that too. On fire and hot."

"What's going on here?" Cat wanted to know, step-ping off the bridge and glancing around to see Tyler be-gin his journey across. "What are we talking about?"

Margie dragged her eyes from Jack. "We're just dis-cussing Jack's bad behavior."

Cat grinned at him and her dark eyes sparkled. She said, "I think your behavior is wonderful. I've always wanted to threaten Tyler."

"You have not," Margie said, frowning at her sister.

"I most certainly have, but I was afraid he would tell Uncle Bonny and you would never get your inheri-tance." She grinned at Jack. "I have mine. I'm the good sister."

Tyler had walked halfway across the bridge when Jack called, "Tyler, let me ask you something. Did you ever get a pinkie ring out of a bubble gum machine and give it to a girl who stood there bawling over it?"

"Stop," Margie urged, touching his arm.

"I'm just curious."

"I have no idea what you're talking about," Tyler told him, pressing on.

Jack smiled at Margie. "I knew he wasn't the man for you."

With everyone safely on the far side of the bridge, the four of them moved on until Margie saw lights shin-ing through a window of a small shack. Palm brush and thicket surrounded the structure. Colorful bottles hung from tree limbs. Margie tapped one. "Obeah."

"What?" Tyler wanted to know, staring at the bottles swinging on a string.

"Obeah. It's the local religion brought over from Africa, I think. The colored bottles are supposed to keep the evil spirits away."

Jack slapped Tyler on the shoulder. "Doesn't seem to be working. You're still here."

Tyler ignored him. "Where do you come up with such nonsense?" he asked Margie.

"Yale," she answered, following Jack to the door. "I took a minor in World Religion."

"You've wasted a lot of time on minors."

"You certainly have," Jack answered beneath his breath and knocked on the door.

A pistol slipped through the curtains of an open window.

"Well, this is just going from bad to worse, isn't it?" said Cat.

A male voice behind the curtain asked, "Who are you?"

Jack explained, "We brought a lawyer for Toho."

Chapter Nine

The door opened to reveal candle sconces on every wall of the one-room shack. A bed sat against a wall and a table fit beneath the window. Toho sat at the table. The two men who had stolen Margie's purse stood at either side of him. Toho asked Tyler, "You're the lawyer? Did you bring the visa?"

"I didn't know you wanted one until I arrived an hour ago."

In the pale light of the room, Tyler's hair looked darker blond. His white shirt turned yellow. "I'm not going to do anything criminal for you."

In the quiet of the woods, Margie heard crickets through the open window. She stood next to Jack who stood next to Cat. The thief, with a cast on his arm, snarled at Margie and she feebly nodded. "Hello."

Toho smiled at Tyler. His teeth glinted in the candlelight and he lifted a hand to reveal Margie's ring still on his pinkie. "Have you forgotten about this?"

Tyler stood straighter. "It's not worth ruining my career."

Jack twisted to whisper in Margie's ear, "He is good, just like you said. Me, I would probably give Toho anything he asks for since there is a gun pointed at us. But that's me."

Toho looked at them. "Why do you whisper and hiss?"

The thief beside him pointed the weapon at Jack.

Margie raised her hands. "Idle chitchat; we'll stop now."

Toho looked at Tyler again. "You don't need the ring? Do you need these?" He pulled Margie's financial papers out of her purse and laid them on the table.

Tyler took one look at the report and turned toward Margie. "You carried these around with you?"

"I had just left the bank," Margie defended, lowering her hands.

"And ran straight to the Bahamas with Jack Ivan?" He said the name "Jack" like it left a vile taste in his mouth.

Margie shrugged at him and then glared at Jack. Now did he see the mess he had gotten her into?

Toho continued, "I don't need a visa when I can have money. You will go to town and have it wired to you. Then you will return here and bring it to me." He looked at Margie.

"Me?"

"Yes, you, and you will return quickly because I have another wedding service to conduct." He stood and placed both hands on the table. "Bring me," he took the papers and stared at the bottom line, "a quarter of what is listed here." Margie did a quick calculation in her head. "No one is going to wire that amount of money. Besides my money is a little tied up . . ."

"You will convince them to wire the money or your friends will suffer for it." He waved his hand at the two men beside him. "Search them."

One of the men patted Jack's shirt pocket. He removed the plane ticket. Jack took his wallet and placed it on the table. Cat removed her watch and handed it to the man with the gun. Tyler emptied his pockets on the table. The thief with the arm cast turned to Margie and pointed at her hand.

"What?" she faltered. "This?" She frowned at her pinkie ring. "It's not worth anything."

"Then you won't mind parting with it," the thief replied, stepping closer. "Give it to me."

Margie faced Toho while keeping a tight hold of her pinkie ring. "This is worthless, really."

The man grabbed Margie's wrist with his good hand.

"You can't have it," she exclaimed, pulling her wrist away.

The ring came off and dropped to the floor. It landed near the table and Margie dropped to one knee.

"Stop her!" Toho barked.

Jack took advantage of the moment, snatched the gun from the other man, and then punched him in the face.

The fellow tumbled backward into the cast-armed

thief, who fell against Tyler. There was much hollering and cursing after that. Chair legs scraped against the wood floors and footsteps pounded. The candle on the table slid against the wall and the curtain there got caught up in the tiny flame. . . .

Margie saw her pink-stoned ring by the leg of the table. She reached for it and then stood just in time for Tyler to knock her sideways. Toho fell backward in his chair when Margie landed in his lap. Her ring slipped from her finger again and rolled toward the bed. She pushed off Toho's twisting body and made a grab for the ring. Feet scuffled in front of her face. Tyler screamed something incoherent as he grabbed the diamond from the old man's finger.

The cast-armed thief kicked Tyler in the side and pulled the diamond from his hand.

To break up the altercation, Jack pointed the weapon above his head and fired four times at the ceiling. The bullets did little damage to the thatched roof that was already starting to smoke from the curtains that were on fire.

"Let's go!" Jack yelled, grabbing Margie's arm and pulling her to her feet.

"My ring!" she insisted, still reaching for it. "I can't leave without my ring!"

Tyler held up the diamond. "I have it!" he announced to the universe.

Toho's bodyguards jumped him and the three of them fell backward onto the table. Tyler twisted and punched the men while using language most improper for a gubernatorial candidate—then he grabbed Margie's arm and pushed her toward the door. Cat ran out after them with her curly ponytail bobbing frantically. Margie lost sight of Jack as Tyler pulled her roughly behind him and into the trees. Where was he? The walls of the shack started to cave. "Jack!" she screamed, pulling out of Tyler's grip. She stumbled forward but Tyler seized her arm again.

Jack emerged from the smoking hut still waving a pistol. He held Margie's purse in his free hand. The two gunmen escaped the house and then made a grab for Jack. The three of them tumbled to the ground.

"We've got to help him," Margie told Tyler.

Tyler pulled on her arm. "Jack is a big boy. He can take care of himself."

Five minutes later it started to rain, and not just a sprinkle like earlier in the day, but a tropical monsoon that doused the house fire and turned the dirt path to mud.

Five minutes later the rain stopped.

Tyler rounded a corner, slipped in the sludge, and dragged Margie down with him. Cat fell against a palm tree and held onto it so that she wouldn't join them in the slime. Her red shirt and jeans clung to her figure like Saran Wrap. "There's the bridge," she said, pointing ahead of them.

Tyler tried to stand, lost his balance, and fell in the mire again. Margie tried to crawl forward but the mud sucked the shoes off her feet. She twisted around and grabbed for them. Tyler looked a bit panicky. "We're in quicksand, aren't we?"

"This isn't quicksand," said Margie, and then more uncertainly, "I don't think." She flung mud from her finger, spraying Tyler's shirt with it.

He looked down at his blotchy white shirt. "We're going to die right here on Little Abaco . . . in quicksand."

Tyler's panic began to drive Margie's panic. "I don't want to die!"

Cat held onto the tree and reached for Margie. "Come on, let me pull you out."

Tyler reached for Cat at the same time as Margie did.

"We're going to die," Cat cried, swimming in the mud beside Margie. Just then, Jack sprinted straight through the mud past them with one hand carrying Margie's purse and the other hand clutching his crucifix. He passed them without a word, dashed through the clearing, and headed for the bridge.

The two Bahamian thieves ran through the mud and raced after Jack. Tyler, Cat, and Margie stared at each other. Obviously, this was not quicksand but only mud. Margie pushed to her feet and raced after Jack. Cat jumped up and followed Margie. Tyler crawled out of the mud and limped along after them.

One of the men chasing him tackled Jack just before he stepped onto the bridge. "Give me the ring!" he shouted.

"You leave him alone!" Margie screamed and kicked the man on top as hard as she could.

"Yooouuu," he snarled and pushed to his feet. "All I want is the diamond," the cast-armed fellow told them.

"I don't have the ring," Jack said.

"He doesn't have the ring," Margie agreed. "Tyler has it."

Tyler Bonaguide stumbled into the clearing. Mud slicked his trousers in long gray streaks. "What?" he asked when he realized everyone was staring at him.

"They want the diamond," Margie told him.

Tyler felt in his pockets and pulled the diamond out of his trousers. Even in twilight the stone found a measure of reflection and twinkled brilliantly. "You want the diamond?" Tyler asked mockingly. "Take the diamond." In a swift stroke, he threw the ring into the gulch.

Without a moment of hesitation the two thieves chased after the twinkling rock and slid down the side of the mountain behind it.

Cat and Margie looked over the side of the slope. Cat said, "They have no dignity at all, do they?"

Margie looked at her, taking note of the slime covering the girl from head to foot. "They should be more like us."

By the time they were back on the ferry, Tyler's face had taken on an ashen look. "I'm completely caked in mud," he mumbled peevishly.

Cat smiled brightly, enjoying his misery.

Margie elbowed her sister and then turned to watch Jack pull the certificate out of her still smoldering purse. The parchment sagged and then disintegrated in his fingers.

Margie took the seat next to him. "I'm sorry, Jack."

The lights on the boat shadowed his sad features. His dark hair was still wet and he had brushed it out of his face with grimy hands. The front locks stuck together with drying mud. A long streak of mud highlighted his cheekbone and the scruffy beginnings of his beard.

He had never looked so wonderful.

Jack swallowed hard and stared at the ocean. Thin wispy clouds dragged over the moon. The rain moved away and a soft but humid breeze started to blow.

"Gee, that's too bad about your document," Tyler said. He sat behind Jack in a chair at another table.

"Stop it, Tyler," Margie told him. "That was an important piece of paper. Jack is upset."

Tyler's face twitched. "But you're not, are you Margie?" He fixed her with an intense look through his wet lashes. "This is all a common occurrence to you, isn't it: thieves, guns, burning buildings, torrential downpours, and quicksand?"

Cat came to her defense. "It's a better life than sitting around in a dull courtroom all day."

Tyler ignored her. "Tell me, Jack. What was so important about the document, hmm? Is there anything I can help you with while I'm just sitting around in a dull courtroom all day?"

Margie caught her breath and looked at Jack. Would he tell Tyler the whole truth and nothing but the truth?

Jack turned to eye Margie with half-closed glittering eyes. He took a breath and turned in his seat to face Tyler. "It's none of your business, Bonaguide."

Tyler laughed, leaned his head back against the railing, and closed his eyes.

Margie held Jack's gaze. "Thank you," she mouthed silently.

Chapter Ten

Back at the Radisson, Uncle Bonny greeted them in the lobby. He stood near the couches in the atrium. He had changed into a blue polo shirt and beige trousers. Looking very sporting, he called, "Tyler, Margie!" When they neared him, he asked, "Did you rescue the engagement ring?"

He didn't seem to wonder about their clothing or their state of disarray. While Tyler explained their adventure, Margie caught sight of Andrew and Brittany near the stairs. Jack saw them too and walked in their direction.

William Walker stood at the end of the couch. "Dad!" Margie called, very happy to see him. Reaching for him, she slid into his arms, mud and all. Cat grinned and joined them. Two people could not look more alike than William and Cat Walker. Both were slender and olive-skinned and dark-eyed. Margie was the odd one out. If she hadn't looked so much like her mother's family she would have suspected she'd been adopted.

But then again, Margie was her father through and

through. His own antics over the years had left him out when his parents willed the trust fund management to Uncle Bonny. Now he held Margie at arm's length. "Morris filled me in. He claims to have pictures of your adventure." He snorted a laugh. "I'm jealous over it. I've never gotten one picture of my adventures."

She broke the bad news to him. "Frierson has been hanging around."

"Ernie Frierson is here?" Cat asked, looking across the lobby. "He gets paid by the photo, right? Who hired him this time?"

"Nobody knows," William answered. "Morris thinks it's one of Tyler's political opponents."

Just then Uncle Bonny cleared his throat. "Excuse me everyone. I've rented a conference room for this evening. We need to have a family meeting."

"Could we clean up a bit?" Margie asked him, longing for a shower.

"There is no time," Uncle Bonny told her and motioned to Jack and then to Brittany and Andrew, who still stood nearby. "I would like you three to join us, if you will. This matter involves you."

The group gathered around Morris Bonaguide. "While I was at the airport waiting for William to arrive, I was approached by a man who wanted to sell me some photographs. If you'll join me in the next room, Mr. Frierson will show them to us."

Ernie Frierson sat at the head of a large rectangular table. He had his projector set up on one end and a large white screen pulled into position on the opposite wall.

"Where's the popcorn?" Cat wanted to know while taking a seat next to Margie.

Tyler sat next to his father. Jack sat next to Brittany and Andrew, who were three seats away from Margie. She realized how unhappy Jack looked when Brittany showed him her wedding ring.

"Let it roll," Uncle Bonny directed.

Ernie happily complied by turning off the lights and switching on the video. The film flickered to life and everyone at the table stared in awe at the scenes unfolding before them.

"What's that fragment right there?" Uncle Bonny asked, tilting his head trying to get a better look.

"That fuzzy thing?" Ernie asked. "It was a close-up of a donkey. Now that warped object there is a dog jumping into the two-wheeler, and the odd shape that flashed by was an umbrella table, and here—"

"Don't you have clearer pictures?" Uncle Bonny insisted.

Frierson fit another DVD into the projector. "Ahh, here we go; the Forty Winks Inn. Margie and Jack shared room two-oh-nine on the night of April first."

Tyler jumped from his chair. "You spent the night with him?" His green eyes blazed in accusation.

"Nothing happened," Jack interrupted.

Frierson continued his narration. "Here, I caught up with Margie Ivan in Nassau. There was some sort of riot and I followed her and Jack to the ferry. We landed on Little Abaco and I traced them to the Civic Hall."

"You looked nice in that muumuu, Ernie," Margie commented warmly.

Frierson tossed her a wry smile.

"Why do you keep referring to Margie as Margie Ivan?" Tyler wanted to know. "Her last name is Walker."

Ernie nodded but didn't answer. Instead, he said, "You'll note the shaman at the front of the room."

"What's a shaman?" Cat asked.

Margie answered, "Witch doctor."

"Ohhh," her sister said while nodding. "He looks like the fellow in the shack."

"He *is* the fellow in the shack," Jack answered.

Tyler asked, "What's he saying?"

"He's performing a wedding," Ernie declared.

Uncle Bonny sat forward. "For all those people?"

"Yes, and you'll notice Margie and Jack in the center of the room." The pictures revealed Jack, taller than most of the men, glancing around the room searching for Brittany. Margie stood paralyzed beside him, staring at Toho.

"The happy bride," Cat observed.

Now Morris Bonaguide jumped to his feet. "*You married Jack Ivan?*" He glared at Margie now with his eyes bulging.

Tyler stared at Margie too. He whispered, "Is it true?"

Margie offered an awkward smile. "I thought I could win a toaster."

Cat shook her head. "I can't count the times you've gotten into trouble over a toaster."

"I know, but I had a good chance at winning this time. The odds were definitely in my favor."

Cat made a face at Margie. "You still own a condo timeshare in Elbow Corners, North Carolina."

"And I'm going to visit one day too."

Tyler cleared his throat. "Margie," he began. "Were you going to tell me about this?"

"Well, of course," she said carefully.

Margie's father stayed seated and stared at the pictures on the screen. He simply blinked at the vast array of photos that Margie later referred to as *What I Did on Spring Break.*

Brittany glared at Jack. "You did it, didn't you? You married Margie. I can't believe it."

"What's wrong with marrying Margie?" Cat asked. "She comes from a very classy family."

Jack looked much brighter now and smiled at Cat and then looked at Andrew McDonald. "I think this is proof enough to keep the decision rights of the Flying D in my name."

"But will it hold up in court?" Andrew asked.

Morris Bonaguide answered him, "You bet it will. I'll make sure it does."

Cat stared at Andrew McDonald. "I don't think that's the most interesting question on the table. Who hired you, Frierson?"

"One of my opponents, no doubt," Tyler answered, refusing to look at Margie.

"Bonaguide hired me," Ernie admitted.

Margie's father sat forward. "Bonaguide?"

"Yes, Morris Bonaguide."

Everyone stared at Tyler's father.

Ernie continued, "He said he was worried about how Margie might affect his son's political career, and I was to make sure I photographed something worth a breakup."

"I hope you got your money before you explained all that," said Cat.

Morris Bonaguide bustled for a moment and then defended himself loudly. "I want to protect Tyler. He is running for governor."

"I think we've all seen those hot commercials," Jack answered, lifting a brow at Margie.

Margie's father stood. "You say you'll protect Tyler at all costs?" He looked tall and square shouldered, and a bit protective while he was at it.

"Of course."

William leaned his hands on the conference table. "Well, it's going to cost you a lot, Morris."

"What do you mean?"

"Since Margie is married now, she is entitled to her entire settlement. I think we'll pay you a visit for a withdrawal on Tuesday or Wednesday."

Bonaguide stood. "That's a lot of money to withdraw from one account, William."

"Oh, we won't withdraw exactly. We'll transfer it to another bank, along with Cat's and mine."

"Here now," Uncle Bonny stuttered. "I never meant to offend. What would your father say?"

William didn't answer. Instead, he bent to kiss Margie on her muddy cheek. "See you tomorrow?"

Margie grinned up at him. "I'll be there as quick as I can."

Morris Bonaguide followed her father out the door. Cat followed them but gave a quick wave to Margie.

"I think we need to talk," Tyler said on Margie's left. He had leaned over the vacant seat and his hazel eyes looked cool and unfriendly.

Margie followed him out the door but turned to see Jack just one last time. He sat with Brittany and Andrew and didn't look up to see her go.

Tyler led the way through the high-ceilinged lobby and then outside to stand by the pool area. No one was around at ten o'clock. Closed umbrellas sat on the table-tops and the chaise lounges were shoved against the wall.

When he turned toward her, Margie caught her breath. She had dreaded this moment. How indifferent Tyler appeared standing with his hands in his pockets. He gazed past her toward the ocean. A breeze moved the palm fronds beyond the iron gates of the pool area.

He spoke, and his voice sounded husky and unemotional. "Who are you, Margie? Do I know you at all?"

"Of course."

"No," he told her, shaking his head. "I thought I knew you. I mean, obviously you are unpredictable. I always thought of you as very charming because of it. And I knew things happened to you sometimes, but I guess I never was involved in any of your escapades.

Seeing it on the big screen, well . . ." He raked his hair back with his fingers. Then he squinted at her. In the soft glow of the night lamps, his features looked shadowed and rough. "Tell me what you were thinking when you ran off with Ivan."

"I was thinking that I didn't want another lawsuit for you to have to defend, Tyler. You're always pulling my family out of trouble for one thing or another and I just didn't want to cause any more problems."

"I'm not always pulling your family out of trouble," he corrected. "I'm always pulling *you* out of trouble. Your father has long since settled down." He turned toward the hotel and looked up at the lights five stories up. "You knew someone would be watching now that I'm running for office."

"Yes, but I didn't expect it to be your father."

"I'm not upset by that," Tyler told her, turning back around to face her. "It doesn't matter who it was that watched you, because you tore off to Miami, spent the night with another man, eloped in the Bahamas . . ."

"Not intentionally."

"And that makes it more suitable?" His next words sounded strained. "Under the circumstances, Margie, I think we should reconsider our wedding plans."

She bit her lip and then said, "I'm sorry about your ring."

He shrugged. "It doesn't matter now." Looking restless, he added, "I need to see about a flight home." He started to walk away but then had an afterthought. He asked, "Will you return to Tampa tomorrow?"

Margie nodded. "I need to see about my car in Miami first. Maybe I can hire someone to fix it and drive it
home for me. There are also some legal issues concerning a Cessna." She gave him a quick smile, trying to
lighten the moment. "I don't suppose you know a good
lawyer?"

Tyler turned to walk toward the gate but called over
his shoulder, "I'm afraid I don't, Margie. Not this time."

Jack looked for Margie the next morning. No wild
pink clothes caught his eye. He searched the hotel, the
straw market, the airport, and the ferry service. Since
her family left early without her, Jack assumed she was
still on the island. Did she leave with Tyler? Would
she?

Jack refused to believe it. Margie loved him. He knew
it as well as he knew he loved her. And he wouldn't return to the Flying D without her. He would search Miami
for her and there he would beg her to marry him—not for
land rights this time, and not for any reason other than he
cherished her. He had loved Margie since the moment
she had said, "Well, if you weren't trying to steal my
purse, then what was the strap doing around your neck?"

Jack bought a ticket for the 11:30 flight to Miami
aboard the seventy-five-seat airbus and sat in an aisle
seat. He fiddled now with the ring he had found for
Margie. It was in his plaid shirt pocket.

His plane missed its departure time and still sat on
the runway at 11:35. He stared out the window. No rain
delayed the flight and he was just about to ask the stew-

ardess what was taking so long when he heard the engine roar to life.

The stewardess offered Jack a drink. He shook his head. Didn't anyone understand? He had to find Margie. It was his only goal, his only desire.

He tried to settle into his seat. The man next to him wore a Rolex and Jack stared at it. In thirty minutes he would be off this plane and in pursuit of Margie. The seat belt sign went off and the passengers began to talk. Jack ignored the voices. He could almost feel Margie near him even though he knew many miles separated them now. He wanted to be alone with his thoughts of her.

But one voice interrupted his contemplation and he twisted around to see who spoke.

"It says here that if the plane goes down, you're supposed to tuck your head between your knees and cover your head with your arms."

Jack stared at Margie in the seat behind him.

She leaned forward and smiled at Jack. "I think we found that panicking, shouting, and kicking the door out works best in that particular situation, don't you think?"

How she came to sit behind him, or when, Jack didn't know. Suddenly, his whole perspective brightened. All the noise in the cabin hushed as he stared at the woman he loved and would always love. Her blonde hair fell gently to her shoulders. She had finally changed out of the flowered pants and into a pair of jeans and a white blouse. Finding his voice, Jack told her, "I searched for you at the hotel. I checked the airport and the police station."

Her emerald eyes searched his. "Why?"

"I—I wanted to give you something."

"Really?" She smiled and her lips parted. "What is it?"

He dug in his pocket and pulled out her pink-stoned pinkie ring he had grabbed on the way out of Toho's shack. "I know this looks cheap, but it brings love that sticks like glue." He twisted around and took her hand to slip it on her finger.

Margie's happy face stared at the ring. "You found it." Then she looked at Jack again.

He saw that she loved him, confirming what he knew. He said, "Marry me, Margie. Again. Don't let me go home alone. I would die of boredom." He kissed her, and neither of them noticed the glances or the murmurings from the other passengers . . . or the flash from a camera that went off two rows back.